THE SAVAGE DAMSEL AND THE DWARF

THE SAVAGE DAMSEL AND THE DWARF

Gerald Morris

Houghton Mifflin Company
Boston

To my parents, Russell and May Morris.

Copyright © 2000 by Gerald Morris

The text of this book is set in Horley Old Style.

Library of Congress Cataloging-in-Publication Data

Morris, Gerald, 1963–
The savage damsel and the dwarf / Gerald Morris.
p.   cm.
Sequel to: The squire, his knight, and his lady.
Summary: Lynet, a feisty young woman, journeys to King Arthur's
court in order to find a champion to rescue her beautiful older sister,
and she is joined in her quest by a clever dwarf and a bold kitchen
knave, neither of whom are what they seem.
RNF ISBN 0-395-97126-8 PAP ISBN 0-618-19681-1
1. Gareth (Legendary character)—Juvenile fiction. [1. Gareth
(Legendary character)—Fiction. 2. Knights and knighthood—
Fiction. 3. Magic—Fiction. 4. England—Fiction.] I. Title.
PZ7.M82785Sav   2000
[Fic]—dc21   99-16457 CIP

Manufactured in the United States of America
RRD 10 9 8 7 6 5 4 3 2 1

"Right so fareth love nowadays, soon hot soon cold; this is no stability. But the old love was not so; men and women could love together seven years, and no licours lusts were between them, and then was love, truth, and faithfulness; and lo, in likewise was used love in King Arthur's days."

—Sir Thomas Malory, *Le Morte d'Arthur*

Contents

PROLOGUE: BEAUMAINS   I

I   LADY LYNET   5

II   ROGER   18

III   THE KITCHEN KNAVE   35

IV   QUESTING   54

V   THE KNIGHT OF THE BLACK WOODS   73

VI   KNIGHTS IN MANY PRETTY COLORS   87

VII   ROGER'S JOURNEY   107

VIII   THE KNIGHT OF THE RED LANDS   125

IX   IN THE OTHER WORLD   135

X   THE NIGHT OF THE HALF MOON   157

XI   GAHERIS'S STORY   176

XII   THE HONOR OF SIR LANCELOT   188

EPILOGUE: THE SAVAGE DAMSEL

AND THE DWARF   208

AUTHOR'S NOTE   211

Prologue: Beaumains

It came to pass in the years of darkness, when magic and sorcery did oppress England, that a great king arose and for a time drove back the evil forces. He was y-clept Arthur, son of Uther Pendragon, and his court was at Camelot. From this great court, noble knights rode out and fought evil wheresomever they found it, be it dragons or be it recreant knights. Thus these knights gained great worship, unless the recreant knights won, which did happen sometimes.

Of Arthur's knights, two were most honored: the king's nephew, Sir Gawain, and the French knight, Sir Lancelot du Lac. And when Sir Gawain rode away seeking adventures, accompanied only by his squire Terence, Sir Lancelot drew all honor unto himself, for he had never been unhorsed by any knight whatsomever.

In due time, Sir Gawain returned, having earned glory, and King Arthur did proclaim a tournament. At this tournament, a strange knight y-clept Sir Wozzell, later considered a wizard, did unhorse Sir Lancelot and then disappeared. In sorrow and shame, then, Sir Lancelot declared he would leave the court and end his days in a forest hermitage, and he departed with great dolor.

At this time arose a young knight, Sir Gareth of Orkney, the youngest brother of Sir Gawain, who did love Sir Lancelot. Sir Gareth vowed that he too would depart, and he swore a solemn oath that ne'er would the court of Camelot hear his name again until he had restored the honor of Sir Lancelot, the greatest of all knights. Thus rendered he much worship to Sir Lancelot.

Sir Gareth's vow grieved the soul of his brother Sir Gaheris, who spoke to Sir Gawain. "Gawain, my brother," quoth Sir Gaheris, "we cannot let our youngest brother expose himself to such danger. The silly sod will get lost before e'er going out of sight of the castle. To speak truth, Gareth hath need of a trail of breadcrumbs to find his own chamberpot."

But Gawain said only that Gareth must fulfill his stupid vow by himself, and so Sir Gareth departed alone on his quest. The next day, Sir Gaheris followed his youngest brother at a distance, ready to succor him *should he lose his way. After Gareth and Gaheris had been gone for a month, and no word had come, then Sir Gawain repented himself of his hardness of heart, and he set off alone to seek his two brothers.*

Many months passed, and still no word came. Then, but a day before Easter, when King Arthur held court most plenour, a strange dwarf appeared at the court, leading a haggard young man. The man was of goodly size, but gaunt and unshaven, and his hair did hang coarsely over his face. The dwarf led the young man to Sir Kai, King Arthur's seneschal, and did request food for him, lest he starve.

"Right gladly," said Sir Kai. Then the dwarf departed alone.

When he was gone, the young man said, "I ask one further boon. Allow me to stay here as a servant."

Then quoth Sir Kai, "If you wish, sirrah. What is your name?"

"That will I not say," replied the young man.

Then Sir Kai laughed. "Why then, I must christen thee myself. I shall call thee Beaumains, which is to say 'Pretty Hands,' for though your appearance is coarse, your hands are soft and your nails betrimmed like unto a lady's — or a courtier's."

At Sir Kai's mockery, the young man was wonderly wroth, for he was none other than Sir Gareth himself, but he hid his face and did not speak for cause of the vow he had taken, that none should speak his name until he had restored the honor of Sir Lancelot. Then took he his place in the kitchen, and soon the court grew used to the kitchen knave whom Sir Kai had scorned, and none wist his true name.

I

LADY LYNET

From the castle wall, Lynet watched the battle with mingled horror and hope, mostly horror. The young challenger was no match for the Knight of the Red Lands, who was obviously toying with him. Even from her place high above the battleground outside, Lynet could hear Red Lands taunting the young knight. At last, wearying of his game, the Knight of the Red Lands knocked his challenger's sword to the ground. The young knight removed his helmet and knelt in submission, according to the chivalric custom of the day, but the Red Knight cared little for custom and less for chivalry. As soon as the young man bowed his head, the Red Knight struck it off, then laughed uproariously, as if he had just done something clever. Lynet looked away, clenching her teeth in helpless fury.

"What, is it already over?" came a jovial voice behind

her. Lynet's uncle and guardian, Sir Gringamore, was just coming up the steps with Lynet's older sister Lyonesse. "This new challenger must have been rather a dud," Sir Gringamore said with a laugh.

"He was just a boy," Lynet said softly.

"Oh, well then, it's better this way," Lyonesse said gaily. "I suppose I will have to marry the champion who rids us of the Knight of the Red Lands, and really, I couldn't marry some nameless boy."

"Certainly not," assented Sir Gringamore. "Wouldn't be up to your consequence, my love."

"He wasn't nameless," Lynet said, fighting back anger. "He was somebody's son, somebody's brother—"

"Oh, you know what I meant," Lyonesse interrupted impatiently. "He just wasn't important enough for the daughter of a great duke, like me."

Lynet knew that it was useless to argue—neither her older sister nor her uncle was capable of feeling compassion for a stranger—but she couldn't restrain herself. "You heartless witch!" she snapped. "That boy gave his life to rescue you! If a man risked his life for me—"

"For you?" Lyonesse retorted. "You don't really expect it, do you? *Dear* plain Lynet!" Lyonesse tittered to herself.

Lynet had no chance to reply, for just then the Knight of the Red Lands called up from the field below. "Are you there, Lady Lyonesse, my pretty? Did you see? I've fought another battle for you! When will you consent to marry me? For your beauty haunts me at night!"

Blushing, Lyonesse leaned over the wall. "Really, Sir Knight, a woman needs time to think these things over!"

"But, my love, it's been six months! And I've killed thirty-six knights already for you. Doesn't that prove anything?"

"Yes!" shouted Lynet, pushing Lyonesse aside. "It proves that you're a scoundrel, a cruel fiend, a beast!" Lynet turned to her sister, "Lyon, why don't you just tell him to go to — Never mind, I'll tell him: Listen to me, you red blister! Go to —"

"Lynet!" shrieked Lyonesse. "What are you doing?"

"I'm getting rid of a plague! You'll never marry that human manure, and you need to tell him so. Maybe then he'll go away!"

"All right, my dear!" the Red Knight shouted from below. "I'll give you more time." The knight mounted his horse and galloped back to his camp, which encircled Lyonesse's home, the Castle Perle.

"That wasn't very clever, Lynnie," remarked Sir Gringamore. "If you make him angry, he'll just attack the castle and take Lyon by force."

Lynet scowled. "I'm just so tired of young knights wearing their father's armor and dreaming romantic dreams riding up to their death."

7

"It *is* a pity that we haven't attracted a better class of rescuer," Lyonesse said with a sigh. "I wish we could get word to King Arthur's court. All the best knights are there."

"You know better than that," Sir Gringamore said. "Arthur won't have forgotten that your father fought in a rebellion against him. The king's more likely to send the Red Knight reinforcements."

Lyonesse sighed in a practiced way. "Then what will become of me?" she said plaintively. Lynet, realizing her sister was moving into her damsel-in-distress mode, hurried away.

It was hard to accept, Lynet reflected as she sat in her room that evening, but Lyonesse was right. The best solution to their situation was to get word to King Arthur's court and ask for some proven knight to come to their defense. Unfortunately, Sir Gringamore was also right. Lynet's father, Duke Idres of Cornwall, had joined in a rebellion against Arthur years before. He had died in the battle, but doubtless the king still held a grudge against the family of a rebel. So, since King Arthur was their best hope, someone had to appeal to the king without revealing who their father was. Lynet made plans for a journey.

First she put on her plainest gown, which was of rather expensive blue silk but had no gaudy embroidery on it to mark it as rich and fashionable, and she dressed her hair in a simple style, appropriate for a maidservant. The Knight of the Red Lands had set up an extensive camp outside the castle gates, complete with pages, squires, and other household servants. If she were to slip through, she would be more likely to escape notice if she looked like a servant. Next, she packed a small bag with some soap, a comb, and a few essentials. She considered taking some food from the kitchen, but stealing food would be hard to explain if she were caught. Besides, the knights errant in the stories never seemed to have trouble finding food on their travels, and anything a knight could do, she could do better. She blew out the candles in her bed-chamber and waited.

When she judged it was around two o'clock, Lynet made her way down to the castle stables. Working by candlelight, she saddled a delicate mare. This took a long time, partly because of the dark but mostly because ladies were not taught how to saddle horses, or to do anything useful, and Lynet had to work from her memory of watching the grooms.

At last, though, she was able to lead the horse to the front gate, raise the portcullis with only a mini-mum of creaking, and slip out of the castle into the open meadow that sloped down from the gate. While all had gone well so far, before she was truly away, she had to get through the Red Knight's camp. Lynet headed straight for a campfire that burned brightly among the tents.

"Who are you, then?" came a creaky female voice from the darkness.

Lynet started violently, dropping her small bag. "I'm...I'm only a servant girl," she stammered, groping in the grass for the bag.

"Not likely," the voice cackled. "Them's flash clothes, a flash horse, and you even talk flash. Escaping from the castle, are ye?"

"No, no!" Lynet gasped. She found her bag and hugged it close, realizing that while she had remembered a comb and a change of undergarments, she had not thought to bring a weapon. "Not at all."

The voice choked with coarse laughter. "Right, then, of course you ain't. You be a maidservant, I reckon. Walking the master's horse, eh?"

"Yes, that's right," Lynet said, grateful for the explanation.

"And the master's horse being all saddled with a lady's saddle, in the middle of the night, is just the way the master wanted it, I reckon." The voice exploded with raucous laughter.

"Shh!" Lynet whispered urgently. "You'll...you'll wake the master!"

This sent the voice off into another paroxysm of laughter, and another voice, gruff and male, interrupted. "What's all this, then? Who's there?"

"Oh, it's just a couple of poor lady's maids, it is. Nothing to concern you, guard," the first voice replied between guffaws.

The guard snorted. "A likely tale. Who are you really?"

Lynet was paralyzed with fear, but the cackling voice answered immediately, "You be too quick for us, I see. No hiding anything from a clever guard like you. We be escaping from the castle there, riding off to King Arthur to ask him if he mightn't like to send a knight to bash your master a bit for us. Could you tell us the way to Camelot?"

Lynet gasped, and her knees felt weak, but the guard only snorted and wheezed with laughter. "Your first story was better. What do you want, then? We've no handouts for the peasantry here."

"Not even a loaf of bread?" the voice said, shifting from its cackling to a whining tone. "It be a long road to Camelot, you see."

The guard laughed again. "You've got a proper gall, you do. All right, here. It's a bit of old biscuit. Take it and be off."

"Thank'ee, lad. You be a gennleman, a true gennleman."

Before Lynet's bemused eyes, a burly guard stepped out of the shadows, handed a flat piece of bread to a slight figure in a long shawl, then waved them on. A small cold hand grasped Lynet's wrist and pulled her sharply forward. She walked — or rather, staggered — through the ring of tents, following the imperious figure that was tugging her along, and before she knew it, the sleeping camp was behind her, and she was concealed in the shadows of the forest.

"There you are," the figure's voice said, with a chuckle. It no longer sounded like an old woman, but rather like a boy or a young man. "Through the camp. Now, if I were you — well, I'm not, of course, since I'm no ninnyhammer — but if I were you, I'd put some distance between myself and them."

"I'm not a ninnyhammer!" Lynet responded sharply.

The figure giggled suddenly. "Did you really think that you might pass for a servant in that silk dress? Oh dear, heaven preserve such innocence. Arthur's at Camelot, which is northeast. Do you know the Pole Star?"

"Who are you?" Lynet whispered breathlessly.

"Never mind that. Do you know the North Star?"

Lynet didn't, astronomy being another useful art that was not taught to ladies, but she said, "Of course I do. Why did you help me?"

The stranger hesitated, then said, "How old are you, Lynet?"

Startled at being called by name, Lynet could only gasp and whisper, "Sixteen."

"I just wanted to see that you saw seventeen. You

know — or rather, you ought to know — you have great potential. We at the Seelie Court have been watching you for some time now. I couldn't see you throw it all away for one mad, misbegotten plan. Now, you just keep the Pole Star ahead of you and a little to your left, and you can't miss Camelot."

"What is the Seelie Court?" Lynet demanded.

But there was no answer, and Lynet was vaguely aware that a presence had been withdrawn, leaving her alone. Dazedly, she mounted her horse, picked out a bright pinpoint of light that might possibly have been the North Star, and set off.

That particular star may not have been the North Star, but it hardly mattered, since during that night of interminable plodding, Lynet followed several different stars. Every time one faded, or she lost track of exactly which star she was following — it was very poor planning on someone's part that every star looked so much like all the others — she would simply choose a new one and hope that this time she was correct.

Her eyes grew heavy, and more than once she almost fell off her mare, but perhaps the one useful skill that ladies were taught was riding, and Lynet was a true horsewoman. By instinct, she was able to stay in the saddle, even when more than half asleep. At last, the sun rose, directly before her, and she guessed that she was far enough from the Knight of the Red Lands that she could rest. She found a mossy bank under a tree and was soon fast asleep.

The sun was high in the sky when she awoke, and she knew she must have slept for hours. She was acutely hungry and spent several minutes casting about for the fruit and berries that she supposed knights errant ate when traveling. Finding nothing that appeared remotely edible, she remounted, thinking some very harsh thoughts about knights errant who ate everything they found and left nothing for the next travelers.

By midafternoon, Lynet had begun to wonder if grass really tasted as bad as people said, and she knew she was hopelessly lost. At last, she came upon a peasant's cottage, where a man and woman were working in a little garden plot. "Excuse me, good people, could you tell me the road to Camelot?"

The woman stood, her face round and smiling. "But of course, dearie. It's the simplest thing in the world."

Lynet sighed with relief. "Oh, thank you. Do I stay on this road?"

The woman looked doubtfully at her husband, who had joined her. He stroked his chin thoughtfully and said, "You can if you like. But you'll need to turn at Hand's Cross."

"She could turn at the old tanner's field," the woman remarked.

"Ay, she could, but the bridge is washed out on the dairy road."

"She could skip the dairy road, though, if she went round the old grove."

"You mean the walnut grove?" asked the man.

"Ay, she could go round that one, too, but I meant the one where the Smith's boy was taken for poaching last winter."

The man snorted. "Nay, with the water so high, she could never get through the ford."

The woman laughed and turned to Lynet. "He's right, of course. The mister knows best, I reckon. You best not go that way."

Lynet blinked and managed to say, "Very well, I won't. Would you . . . could you tell me which way would be better, please?"

"Look here," the man said in a businesslike voice, "if you want to stay on this road, you best turn at Hand's Cross."

"Where is Hand's Cross, please?" Lynet asked.

"Just past Old Barn Meadow."

"Old Barn Meadow," Lynet repeated.

"Then, a mile after you turn, you'll look for a big oak tree. Go about three furlongs past the oak, then turn again, at the house where the steward used to live."

"Not the present steward, mind you," the woman

interrupted. "It was the old steward who lived there, before it burned."

"The house is burned now?" Lynet asked helplessly.

"Oh, ay," the man agreed. "That would be eight, ten, year ago now."

"No," the woman said. "It would have to be more than that, because Thomas was still at home then. That was the same summer he broke his leg."

"Couldn't be!" the man protested. "When I was taking him to the village to have it set proper, I remember stopping and passing the time of day with the old steward . . ."

Lynet prodded the mare and trotted on, resigned to her fate. After she died of starvation, her body would be found by a band of overfed knights errant in the grove where somebody had been caught poaching.

The sun was low in the sky, and Lynet was faint and famished, when she smelled the unmistakable aroma of roasting meat. Senses sharpened by hunger, she followed the smell to a small copse. There she glimpsed a campfire, with a haunch of venison roasting over it on a stick. She dismounted and lurched toward the food. She was largely indifferent to danger, but she had enough presence of mind to pick up a large branch to use as a club if the owner of the meat was unfriendly. Holding the club in front of her, she stepped to the edge of the small clearing where the meat dripped and sizzled. No one was there.

Lynet looked quickly around, seeing nothing, but her eyes were drawn irresistibly back to the roasting meat. Just as she was about to step out of the shadows and help herself, a flickering shadow to her right caught her eye. From a small bush where she had not thought a man could be concealed sprang a dark figure, and Lynet glimpsed a long sword. Instinctively raising her club, she felt a solid jolt as the sword buried itself in the wood. Lynet leaped backward and felt the sword, still embedded in her branch, pull free from its owner's grasp. Frantically, Lynet grasped the sword by the handle and jerked it free from the wood. Holding the sword before her, she whirled and faced her assailant.

It was a dwarf, bearded and stocky and dressed in ill-fitting clothes. The dwarf staggered backward to escape the sword in Lynet's hand, tripped over a root, and sat heavily. "Why, you're a lady!" the dwarf gasped.

"Don't think I won't use this sword, though," Lynet snapped.

The dwarf ignored her. "A lady," he repeated. "I've just been disarmed and taken prisoner by a lady." He shook his head slowly. "I really am pathetic," he moaned.

II

ROGER

Lynet gripped the sword with both hands and pointed
it at the seated dwarf. Her hands trembled slightly, and
to hide the shaking, she waved the sword threatening-
ly. "Answer me, if you value your life!" she snapped.

"Oh, I value my life," the dwarf replied quickly.
"What do you want to know?"

"Are you alone?"

"Yes, I'm alone." The dwarf frowned at the darkness behind Lynet. "Are you?" he asked.

"I don't have to tell you anything!"

"No, that's true," the dwarf agreed. "Forget I asked.
How else may I help you?"

Lynet said gruffly, "Give me some of that food!"

The dwarf grinned slowly, and though his face had
the heavy, large-featured character of most dwarfs,
Lynet could see his eyes twinkle engagingly in the

firelight. "So, I was right," he murmured. "You *are* a bandit! A savage brigand."

Lynet felt a stir of amusement, and she let her expression soften. "Pardon me, sir dwarf. May I please share your dinner?"

"That you may, my lady. Indeed, you may even set down the sword while you eat. I won't attack you again. Terribly sorry about that. Bad manners to kill ladies, you know." The dwarf stood and bowed stiffly.

Lynet lowered the sword, a smile growing on her face. She had not known many dwarfs, but the ones she did know were notable for their lack of humor. This wry little man with the laughing eyes was different, and instinctively she trusted him. While the dwarf set about taking the meat from the fire, she brought her mare through the bushes and picketed her beside the dwarf's horse. Behind her, the dwarf cried out "Ouch!" and swore vigorously. Lynet glanced over her shoulder at the dwarf, who was dancing around the steaming haunch and blowing on his fingertips.

"Is it hot enough?" Lynet asked innocently.

"Just touch it right here and see for yourself, why don't you?" the dwarf retorted.

"No, that would be stupid," Lynet said. "I might burn myself."

Casting her a baleful look, the dwarf sawed off a chunk of venison and handed it to her on a bent metal plate. Lynet ate ravenously, and only after her third helping did the pangs in her stomach subside enough for her to think of anything else. The dwarf, who had finished his meat long before, was leaning against a rock, watching her.

"The meat's burned," Lynet said.

The dwarf nodded. "Ay, that would be why you just picked at your food."

Lynet tried to look dignified, but without success. "I was hungry," she said.

"You don't say. Have another plate?" Lynet nodded, and the dwarf began hacking the blackened meat again. "It is a bit overdone, I suppose," he said.

"I thought all dwarfs were good cooks."

"And I thought all ladies were too polite to comment on someone else's cooking." Lynet blushed, and the dwarf handed her the meat. She began to gnaw on the venison, and the dwarf said, "Do you mind telling me what you're doing alone in this country?"

Lynet hesitated, but decided to tell the truth. "I'm on my way to Camelot."

"Are you now? Where from?"

"Cornwall. I live in the Castle Perle. You wouldn't know it, but—"

"Heard of it. Isn't that where the old duke, Idres, lived?"

Lynet nodded, watching the dwarf warily, but he said nothing about Idres's part in the old rebellion against King Arthur. Maybe that revolt had been forgotten, she thought hopefully. The dwarf was more concerned about geography, it seemed. "If you're going from Cornwall to Camelot, why are you so far east?"

"I have my reasons!" Lynet said with dignity.

"Got lost, did you?" the dwarf said. "Well, I've no wish to go to Camelot, but I've nothing better to do. I'll take you there."

Lynet lifted her chin. "I won't trouble you," she said haughtily. "I can find my way." The dwarf grinned and cocked one amused eyebrow. Lynet sighed and lowered her chin. "No, I can't. I accept your kind offer, sir — What is your name?"

The dwarf scratched his chin and said, "Roger. Call me Roger."

"Very well, Roger," Lynet replied. "I am Lady Lynet of Perle."

Roger grinned at the title, and unrolled his blankets. "Good night, Lady Lynet of Perle."

Her stomach full at last, Lynet realized how exhausted she was. She pulled her cloak and a blanket around her and lay down. Before she went to sleep, though, she said, "Roger?" The dwarf grunted, and she said, "I'm sorry I was rude. Thank you for offering to help me."

"You're welcome, my lady," came the dwarf's muffled voice.

"And Roger?"

"Mm-hmm?"

"Will you show me which one is the North Star?"

The dwarf chuckled. "Yes, my lady. Tomorrow night."

The next morning, after finishing the venison for breakfast, Lynet and Roger set off. Lynet was some-what self-conscious when she awoke, unsure what she would say to this abrupt little man for the next few days, but then Roger scolded her for saddling the mare wrong, and in the ensuing brangle, all restraint disappeared.

"How do you know which way to go?" Lynet asked as they began. "You can't see the North Star in the daytime."

Roger thought before answering. "There are a few tricks to use — look at the mossy sides of trees, check the direction of the sun, and so on — but that's not really what I do. When I go somewhere, I'm always putting the land in a little map in my head. I don't believe I've ever been lost in the daytime, or on a clear night."

"I suppose women are different that way." Lynet sighed.

"Don't make yourself so special," the dwarf said with a snort. "As if getting lost was some trick that only women knew. I've known men who could get lost in their own bedrooms. The only difference is that men with no sense of direction don't brag about it, the way women do."

Lynet clamped her lips shut, offended but not really angry. Along with her resentment at being criticized, she felt an irrepressible urge to laugh, and for once in her life she was able to stifle a sharp reply.

Roger paid no attention to her silence. As they rode, he pointed out landmarks and directional guides. Lynet did not answer, but she listened attentively, and soon began to notice these markers herself. Finally, as they skirted a stand of trees, Lynet forgot to be aloof and asked, "Did we just change direction? Aren't we going more west than we were?"

Roger grinned slowly. "Ay, my lady. Just to get around this copse. Then we'll change back."

Lynet smiled. "It's not so hard after all," she said.

"I've never found it so. Have you decided you can talk to me now?"

Lynet decided to act dignified. She lifted her chin and said, "Was there something you wished to discuss, my good dwarf?"

Roger chuckled. "No, ma'am. Me, I just like to hear how you great ladies talk. It do be so fine."

As Lynet laughed, it occurred to her that until this mocking lapse into country dialect, Roger's speech had been cultured and educated. In many ways, he was a strange dwarf indeed.

Roger continued. "But I *was* wondering what takes you to Camelot."

Lynet decided to be frank. "I need help," she explained. She told Roger about her sister and how the Knight of the Red Lands was trying to force her into marriage. "I'm going to ask the king if he will send a knight to our rescue."

Roger murmured, half to himself, "So you're Idres's daughter, eh?"

Lynet watched the dwarf's face intently. "Yes. What of it?"

The dwarf raised his eyebrows with faint surprise. "Why, nothing at all. I've heard he was a good man is all."

"I beg your pardon," Lynet said gruffly. Then, quietly, she added, "He was."

Roger nodded and said, "Well, your timing is good. It's almost Whitsuntide. Arthur'll be having a feast and hearing requests. He's sure to send someone along to help you."

Lynet lapsed into thoughtful silence. Evidently the dwarf did not know that Duke Idres had rebelled against Arthur, which was good, but Lynet could not believe that Arthur had forgotten. She would still have to hide her identity at court. But would any knight be willing to ride off with a woman who wouldn't tell her name?

Roger laughed suddenly. "In fact, if what you say is true, you may have the pick of the crop. It isn't every day that a knight gets to rescue a damsel in distress who is not only beautiful — you did say she was a looker, didn't you? — but who owns a castle. Quite a catch."

Lynet's face cleared. "That's right." Maybe her job would be easier than she had thought.

An hour later Lynet began to feel hungry, and said so to Roger.

"You just forget about it," he said. "We finished off my food at breakfast."

"Can't we stop while you hunt some more?"

"I'm a terrible hunter."

"I thought all dwarfs were great archers," Lynet said with surprise.

"And I thought all ladies had small appetites."

Lynet laughed. "Only in public. How did you get that venison that we ate last night?"

Roger grinned, a little sheepishly. "I traded for it. I saw a huntsman with a deer and swapped him a new hunting knife for the haunch."

"So what can we eat?" Lynet asked.

Roger stopped his horse and looked pensively at Lynet for a moment. "I've been thinking about that, and I have an idea, but I'm not sure we can carry it off. Put your cloak on."

"Why?"

"I need to see if you can pass as a man or boy. We're lucky you're well built."

Lynet, who had never been especially taken with her large frame, at least in comparison to her willowy older sister, muttered, "Oh yes, lucky." She put on her long traveling cloak and pulled the hood low over her face.

Roger nodded slowly. "It might work; the cloak is long enough to cover your dress, too. All right, listen to me. About an hour from here, there's a secret camp. Only knights and their servants are permitted there, and no lady has ever seen it. There will be food there, and we can spend the night, but you have to promise me that you won't say a word or take off your hood."

Lynet nodded, but she was puzzled. "Even if I pass as a boy, you're not a knight or a knight's servant," she pointed out.

Roger blinked. "Oh, yes. Well, I used to be. I think they'll let us stay. They're good men, and generous."

The dwarf seemed so confident that Lynet accepted his word without question. She was less certain, though, when they finally drew near to the camp, an hour later. They had for some time been riding through dense forest, and Lynet was hopelessly lost again.

"What do you want?" a curt voice growled at them suddenly. Lynet jumped but did not make a sound.

"Two travelers, seeking the Knight's Sabbath," Roger said calmly.

"Your names?" came the voice again.

"I am Roger the dwarf, lately servant to Sir Gaheris, who directed me here. I bring with me a young penitent. He is on pilgrimage to the shrine of Our Lady of Anglesey, where his family hopes his deafness may be healed."

The voice became much friendlier. "Gaheris, eh? Come in, come in, Master Dwarf. We've been wondering about old Gary." Roger led Lynet out of the trees into a small clearing in the very heart of the forest. Several men lay sprawled around a large, cheerful fire. In the shadows near the trees were tethered some horses, and near the horses was a loose pile of armor.

The man who had challenged them in the forest stepped into the light, and Lynet saw a clean-shaven young man with a bright, open face. "Hey, fellows, here's a dwarf who says he's been with Gaheris," he called.

"Have you, now?" said a man with a thin brown beard and keen eyes. "You are fortunate to have served so skilled a knight. A very wizard with a sword, Sir Gaheris is."

Roger bowed slightly. "Your worship must be thinking of a different Sir Gaheris, I'm afraid. The one I know has many gifts, of course, but his swordsmanship... well, he could use practice."

The knights gave a shout of laughter, and the one with the brown beard grinned broadly. "That's the chap, all right. Forgive me for testing you. Sit down, friend, and tell us how Gary's doing. Did he ever catch up to that cloth-headed brother of his?"

"Has there still been no word from Sir Gareth?" Roger asked, clearly surprised. He frowned, then shrugged and said, "I left Sir Gaheris several months ago, and I've heard nothing. I am now serving as guide to this deaf and dumb boy. Sir Gaheris had told me that should I ever need food and shelter, I would find both at the Knight's Sabbath. With your permission, I and my young charge will sit behind you and share your repast."

The knight with the brown beard chuckled. "A most civil—and educated—dwarf it is! Who taught you to speak so gently? Gaheris?" Roger nodded, and the knight bowed deeply. "Well, sir, you are welcome to what bounty we have, for the love of your master."

Soon Roger and Lynet, still hidden in her cloak, were positioned securely in the shadows away from the fire. At first, Lynet could concentrate on nothing but the plate of food the knights had given her, but when she was at last full, she began to listen to the knights' conversation.

"Say, have we finished off all the boar?" a portly knight by the fire asked. "We need to send out our great hunter to fetch us another one. How about it, Blueberry?"

A knight with a black beard belched loudly and said, "Anything you want, Saggy. But you have to promise to stay in camp, so I don't take you for a fine fat hog and spear you by mistake."

The knights laughed, and the portly one sniffed. "By mistake is the only way you'll ever lay a spear on me, lad." The knights laughed again.

Lynet leaned close to Roger and whispered, "Did they just call that knight 'Blueberry'?"

Roger frowned at her to be silent, but a moment later he whispered, "His real name is Sir Bleoberis. The chubby one is Sir Sagramore the Desirous."

"'The Desirous'?"

"It's a joke," Roger explained. "There's no knight more contented than Sir Sagramore. Good knight, though, when he bestirs himself."

"I'll lay you odds I unhorse you in the next tournament," Sir Bleoberis called to Sir Sagramore.

"What? Is there a tournament coming? Heavens, I must make plans to be away," Sir Sagramore said with alarm. "Anyone hear of any great adventures I could be off to?"

The knights roared with laughter. "What sort of adventures are you looking for, Saggy?" asked the young knight who had encountered Roger and Lynet in the forest.

"That's Sir Harry le Fise Lake," Roger whispered to Lynet.

Sir Sagramore struck a noble pose. "Something perilous, something splendid—"

"Something you can do from a sitting position," interrupted the knight with the brown beard. ("Sir Dinadan," whispered Roger.)

"I did hear of one adventure," said Sir Bleoberis. "Not far from Londinium, there's a chap holding a tournament. The winner gets to marry his daughter."

Sir Harry gave a low whistle. "Thanks for the warning. What do you think's wrong with her?"

"Probably squints," Sir Sagramore said.

"Or has spots," suggested Sir Dinadan. "Best steer clear of Londinium, fellows." The other knights nodded in agreement.

"Now now, Dinadan," Sir Bleoberis said with a grin, "she's probably a very nice girl, one that you'd be proud to show your mother."

"Not I," replied Sir Dinadan. "I've sworn off women. Nothing but a take-in, as Sir Dinas the Seneschal found out. Have you lads heard the tale?" The others shook their heads, and settled themselves comfortably to listen.

Sir Dinadan cleared his throat and began. "In Cornwall, where King Mark ruleth, abideth a passing good knight who is y-clept Sir Dinas—"

"Stow it, Dinadan!" interrupted Sir Harry, laughing. "Just tell us what happened and save the foofaraws for the minstrels."

Sir Dinadan grinned and continued in a more natural tone. "Seems that Sir Dinas loved this lady. Gave her the best rooms in his castle, gave her everything. But she made a rope out of her towels, climbed out the window, and ran away with another knight."

"Strumpet," Sir Sagramore commented, to no one. "He's better off without her."

"Not so, my jaded friend," replied Sir Dinadan. "When she left, she took along two of Sir Dinas's best hunting dogs, the finest brachets in Cornwall."

Sir Bleoberis grew suddenly animated. "She took his hunting dogs? That's too much, dash it! What did Dinas do?"

"He rode after them. He caught up the next day and challenged the knight. Dinas isn't bad for a Cornish knight, and he killed the chap right there. The woman got all starry-eyed and simpered to Dinas about how wonderful he was and how glad she was he'd rescued her, but Dinas just took his dogs and went home."

The knights laughed coarsely. "Left her in the forest, did he?" crowed Sir Harry. "Good man!"

"Were the dogs all right?" asked Sir Bleoberis.

Lynet listened in indignant silence. While she could not approve of the lady's secret affair, she could easily imagine herself in the woman's place, left alone and friendless in the forest with her lover's corpse. She was astonished at these knights' callousness.

"You say this Dinas was a good fighter, eh?" Sir Harry commented. "I didn't think there were any good knights in Cornwall."

"There aren't many, and that's a fact," Sir Dinadan agreed. "But they're not as bad as all that. I think they have a bad reputation because their king is such a bleeder."

"Is King Mark as bumbling as they say?" Sir Bleoberis asked.

Sir Dinadan grinned and glanced into the shadows where Roger and Lynet sat. "Maybe our dwarf can help us with that. I heard that King Mark was un-horsed by old Gaheris. Is that so?"

Roger nodded. "S'truth," he said. "I was there."

"Good Gog," said Sir Sagramore. "This Mark must be blind and crippled, then. Unhorsed by Gary! I could never hold my head up again."

The knights continued talking around the fire, telling stories, laughing good-naturedly at themselves and others. Lynet wrapped up in her blankets and lis-tened, alternately shocked and amused by their casual attitude toward each others' feelings. No matter how they insulted each other, no one ever seemed to take offense. How differently a group of ladies would act, she reflected as she went to sleep.

The sky was still dark, and the stars still bright when Roger woke Lynet and indicated with gestures that it was time to go. Wordlessly, she helped Roger saddle the horses, then mounted and followed the dwarf out of the forest. Only after they had ridden for almost half an hour did Roger speak. "Sorry to wake you so early, but I thought it would be best if we were gone before the others awoke. Less chance they'd spot you for a lady." Lynet nodded, and Roger added, "Though they might not have guessed anyway, from how silent you were. You did very well in there, holding your tongue."

"You mean that you thought all ladies talk too much?"

The dwarf laughed. "I must admit that you are a surprising lady."

"And you," said Lynet, "are a surprising dwarf. You don't act or talk like a dwarf, you know. Even that Sir Dinadan noticed it. And how is it that you seem to know all of them so well, but they didn't recognize you?"

Roger did not look at her. "No one notices a dwarf," he said at last.

The dwarf's voice was wistful, and Lynet tactfully changed the subject. "What did you call that place? The Knight's something?"

"'The Knight's Sabbath'," Roger said quickly. "It's a secret resting place for knights errant. They go out to seek adventures, which is deucedly uncomfortable and not always so easy—adventures don't grow on every tree—and after a while they get tired of it. Then they go to the Knight's Sabbath. There they hunt all day, talk all evening, and make up stories of their great adventures to tell when they go home."

"But that's terrible!" Lynet exclaimed.

Roger turned his short, stocky body and looked at

her seriously. "Why? None of those men back there ever really wanted to be a knight. Not one of them enjoys fighting, jousting, rescuing damsels, and so on."

"Why did they become knights, then?" Lynet asked.

"What choice do they have?" Roger asked. "They're all younger sons: born into noble families but without any real inheritance. What's left for them but to become knights?"

Lynet shook her head. "I still think they're horrid. All these high and mighty knights sitting in a circle saying mean things about knights who aren't even there — like this one that you used to serve."

"Who? Gaheris? They said nothing about him that they wouldn't have said to his face." Roger smiled. "I'm sure Gaheris knows he's a rotten fighter."

"Well, what about those terrible things they said about ladies?" demanded Lynet.

Roger smiled more widely. "I wondered if that would rankle."

"It was awful! Aren't knights supposed to swear some oath to honor ladies?" Roger shrugged, and Lynet shook her head decidedly. "I'm glad I'm going to King Arthur's court. Surely the Knights of the Round Table will be more chivalrous."

Roger swiveled in his saddle and stared at her, amusement growing in his eyes. "Didn't you know?" he asked. "Every one of those knights back there was a fellow of the Round Table."

III

THE KITCHEN KNAVE

"There it is," said Roger, reining in. "On the top of that hill. Camelot." Lynet stared at the towering castle where King Arthur held court and felt suddenly very small. For the first time she was struck with the effrontery of her whole project: she, the sixteen-year-old daughter of a former enemy of Arthur's, had come to his great court seeking aid. For a wild moment, she wondered about going home, and to make matters worse Roger wheeled his horse and said, "I'll be leaving you now. Even you should be able to find your way from here."

"You're leaving?" Lynet gasped, too stunned even to resent his slur on her sense of direction. "Won't you go in with me?"

Roger smiled a lopsided smile and shook his head. "Nay, you've no use for me now."

"But what will I do? How can I see Arthur? Where do I go?"

The dwarf looked at her sharply. "You're not frightened, are you?"

Lynet mustered her self-composure. "Don't be a dolt. Of course not."

Roger grinned. "That's the dandy. I've no doubt you can brazen your way into anywhere you like."

Lynet felt her courage returning. She lifted her chin and said with dignity, "I should be pleased if you would accompany me, all the same."

Roger hesitated, but at last he shrugged. "Oh, very well. But as soon as you're in, I'm off, do you hear?"

Lynet was too relieved to argue, and they rode on together. As they approached the front gate, a hulking guard in chain mail barred their way. "'Old!" he announced gruffly. "No one allowed inside until after Whitsuntide."

"But it is for the feast that we have come," Lynet replied with outward calm.

"Ay, you don't have to tell me that. Come with another problem for the king to solve. You'd think 'is 'ighness 'ad nothing better to do with 'is time than to listen to a parcel of complainers."

Lynet's eyes flashed. "That, sirrah, is exactly what I think! Is he the king of this land or not? Then he shall hear of the abuses that take place in it!" She urged her horse forward, but the guard blocked her

36

with his great spear.

"Not so fast, missy. Sir Kai's orders were to close the gates to newcomers. The king 'as more than enough to muddle with already."

"You forget yourself, guard," Roger said softly. "Speak respectfully to the lady."

"'o! A gnat!" The guard laughed. "What'll you do? Bite my ankle?"

A new voice, calmer and with more authority, intervened. "What's going on here, Colin?"

The guard stood sharply to attention. "More people wanting to see the king, Captain!"

A tall guard with grave eyes stepped up behind the guard. "Very well, Colin. I'll take care of this now." He turned to Lynet and said, "I apologize for my guard's rudeness, my lady, but he only did as he was told. So many have come to ask boons of the king that we can scarce house them all. We are not to permit any new arrivals."

Lynet's heart sank, and she lowered her eyes.

"Nay, my lady," Roger breathed, almost too softly to hear. "Don't give up so soon."

Again, she felt a new courage, as if the dwarf were willing her to be strong. She looked into the captain's eyes. "I will not go away for your convenience. No, not even for the king's convenience! Who is here to serve whom?"

The captain's brows lifted, and a smile lit his eyes.

"I can ask Sir Kai in person, I suppose. If you will give me your name—"

"I will not!" Lynet declared.

"Eh?" said the captain and Roger together.

"I am one of the king's subjects, and I have come to ask his help. That should be enough." She met the captain's gaze squarely.

The captain glanced once at Roger. "Do you know this formidable lady, friend?"

"Somewhat. That's not to say I understand her, mind you." Lynet felt Roger's eyes on her, and she flushed, but she kept her gaze on the captain.

"She will not be sent away, will she?" the captain asked.

"Nay. Of that much I am sure," Roger replied.

The captain grinned. "I think I know what to do, my lady. I'm going to take you to one of the court damsels—she is close to the king and to several of his knights. I rather think she'll like you, and she may be able to help. Would you please follow me?" The captain bowed and led the way across the great bustling courtyard. All around her, Lynet was aware of a festive throng in bright clothes, and she longed to gaze at it in open-mouthed wonder, but mindful of her dignity, she kept her eyes straight ahead.

"Why, there she is now!" the captain exclaimed. "Pardon me! Pardon me, Lady Eileen!"

A short woman in a green dress who had been

38

striding briskly across the court stopped in her tracks. "What is it, Alan?" Then she turned her eyes toward Lynet. Meeting the woman's bold, straightforward gaze, Lynet knew at once that she had found a kindred spirit. She sighed with relief and turned to speak to Roger. The dwarf was gone.

"These are my rooms," Lady Eileen said. "Come in at once and sit down. You've been traveling all day, haven't you?"

"Yes, my lady," Lynet said meekly.

"None of that, now. You'll call me by my name, which is Eileen. Flora! Flora, where are you! Come in here!"

A maidservant bustled in, carrying a dress. "Oh, my lady, I was sure you'd be late. I've brought —"

"No time for that now. I've a guest. I need you to go to the kitchens and bring up food for two. The best of everything. I'll be dining here this evening with my friend."

"But, my lady, the banquet!" the maidservant gasped.

"I suppose it will go on without me," Lady Eileen said indifferently. "Mind you hurry, now. My friend has been traveling far."

Lynet tried to intervene. "No, my lady...I mean Lady Eileen...you mustn't miss a banquet on my account. Indeed, I couldn't —"

"Nonsense. We'll be much more comfortable in here by the fire. Horrid banquet hall is always freezing, even in May. Well, Flora? What are you waiting for?" The maidservant started nervously and scampered from the room. Lady Eileen turned her eyes to Lynet and looked at her quietly for a moment. "I suppose you'd better tell me all about it," she said. "To begin with, what is your name?"

Lynet returned Lady Eileen's gaze, but forlornly. "Must I tell?"

"It is customary. Is there a reason you should not?"

Lynet nodded. "I . . . I wish I could. I don't like to hide. But I'm not here for my own sake, and . . . if I . . ." she trailed off helplessly.

"Never mind," said Lady Eileen. "Can you tell me your story without using names?"

Relieved, Lynet told about her sister and about the siege by the Knight of the Red Lands.

"I see," said Lady Eileen, when Lynet had finished. "And you've come to ask Arthur to send a champion to fight the Red Knight?"

Lynet started to speak, but was interrupted by the arrival of Flora, followed by a serving man, bringing their food. While the serving man laid out a dozen or so plates of enticing food, Lynet answered, "That's right. And my sister will marry the knight who delivers us."

Lady Eileen raised one eyebrow. "Of course she

will," she murmured. "And no doubt your sister is the fairest damsel in all England."

Lynet looked at her sharply. "Oh, dear. You make it sound so ordinary."

"Every damsel in distress is the fairest in all England, it seems," Lady Eileen said drily. "Truthfully, now. Is your sister even passably good-looking?"

Lynet nodded vigorously. "She really is. Flawless. A little wispy thing with mournful eyes and a trembling smile. Besides," she added prosaically, "she's rich. She owns our castle and all the best farmland in our region."

Lady Eileen looked at the serving man, who had finished laying out the meal. "Thank you, Beaumains. That will be all." The kitchen knave left, and Lady Eileen said musingly, "How unusual! A maiden in need who is really beautiful!" She smiled ruefully at Lynet and added, unexpectedly, "And how dreadful for you. I should hate to have a gorgeous sister."

Lynet dimpled. "It *is* trying, sometimes."

"I imagine so. I don't suppose she's the sort who will get sadly overweight when she grows older, is she?"

"No such luck," Lynet replied mournfully. "She'll still be stunning when she's...oh! I didn't mean to say that!" Lynet put a hand to her mouth, but Lady Eileen's eyes held so much understanding that Lynet began to giggle. "I don't really wish her ill, but it's true that I used to daydream about the day when she would be fat and peevish looking. She hardly eats anything, though, and I had to give it up."

"Don't give up," said Lady Eileen reassuringly. "She'll be skinny and peevish looking, and that's even worse. Shall we eat?"

"Yes, please," Lynet said, and for some time they devoted their attention to their meal.

When at last they were both satisfied, Lady Eileen leaned back in her chair and said, "So, if I understand you, you need one of Arthur's knights, but you're afraid that if you tell who you are, then he won't send one. Right?" Lynet nodded. "But you have no other recourse. This Knight of the Red Laundry or whatever it is has bottled you up in your castle—" She trailed off and asked suddenly, "How did you get out, by the way?"

Lynet shook her head doubtfully. "I'm not really sure, myself. I made a plan to escape at night—I was going to pretend to be a maidservant and walk right through the Red Knight's camp—but it never would have worked."

"I shouldn't think so," Lady Eileen said. "You walk with too much assurance. So what happened?"

"That's what I don't understand. Someone met me at the edge of the camp and helped me. At first, it was an old woman—"

"At first?" Lady Eileen interrupted.

"Yes. She... she changed later." Lynet sighed. "I'm afraid this sounds like nonsense."

"Not at all," replied Lady Eileen. "I'm suddenly very interested."

"Well, the old lady convinced the guard that we were local peasants, and then she became a young man, and she... he said he was from the... I've forgotten the name, from some court. It wasn't from Arthur's Court."

Lady Eileen's eyes were bright. "Was it perhaps the 'Seelie Court'?"

"Yes! That's it!" Lynet exclaimed. "What is the Seelie Court, please?"

"The Seelie Court is the world of the faeries, or rather the good part of it. The monsters—hags and ogres and such—are the Unseelie Court."

Lynet stared. "You mean that I was helped by a faery?"

"I do. And if the Seelie Court has taken an interest in you, then I'll certainly do what I can to help."

Lynet started to thank her, but a flicker of motion to her left caught her eye, and a new voice said, "I've just come to see where you... oh, I beg your pardon. I didn't know you were entertaining." Lynet turned to see a young man with a smooth, triangular face and high, arching eyebrows. He stood beside the window, through which he evidently had just noiselessly entered.

Lady Eileen stood. "Come in, Terence. I was just wishing for you. Sorry I missed the banquet. Was it dreadful?" The young man grinned and nodded. Lady Eileen explained, "I was dining with a friend. My friend, this is Terence, squire to Sir Gawain."

Lynet managed not to gape, but she was impressed nevertheless. Sir Gawain's exploits were legendary, and to encounter even his own personal squire left her a little awestruck. But when she looked into the squire's eyes, she forgot about his famous master. This Terence had the brightest and clearest eyes she had ever seen, and he looked at her with keen interest. Raising one eyebrow, he bowed with rare grace and said, "I am your servant, my lady. May I ask your name?"

Lynet did not hesitate. For reasons that she could not explain, she knew that she could neither lie nor hide from this man. "My name is Lynet, sir," she said softly.

Lady Eileen stared, but Squire Terence only smiled with pleasure. "Of course. I have heard of you, my lady."

"You have?" Lynet asked.

"A friend was telling me about you the other day. He said you had great potential, and I see he was right. You have the look."

Lady Eileen smiled brightly and said, "Splendid! I knew she was a right one! Terence, we need to rid her

44

of a knight who's plaguing her castle. Have you heard from Gawain?"

Terence shook his head. "Not in weeks. I suppose he's still looking for his two missing brothers."

Lady Eileen frowned. "That's a nuisance. She needs a good knight, not a painted puppet."

Terence turned toward Lynet. "I'll talk to Sir Kai. He's Arthur's seneschal, and he manages Camelot. He can arrange tomorrow's schedule so that you see the king early."

"Thank you," Lynet said faintly. Terence bowed again.

"And Terence," Lady Eileen added. "Don't mention her name, please."

Terence smiled at Lady Eileen, then disappeared through the window in a single, fluid motion. "Who is he?" she breathed.

"I told you," Lady Eileen replied. "He is Gawain's squire." Lynet shook her head, and Lady Eileen added, "You can trust him, you know. But you do know, don't you? He'll arrange things."

If Lynet had been asked to describe a formidable knight, she would have described someone like Sir Kai. When Squire Terence introduced her to him the next morning, a sense of relief swept over her. Sir Kai had great brawny arms and an air of complete assurance.

Though his black beard was flecked with gray, there was no comparison between this great warrior and the callow, half-hearted young knights Lynet had seen at the Knight's Sabbath. "This the lady?" Sir Kai growled at Squire Terence.

Terence nodded to Sir Kai, smiled reassuringly at Lynet, then disappeared into the crowd. Sir Kai led her to a seat in the great hall, and then Lynet was free to gaze with awe at the splendor about her: men in bright clothes and long, curled shoes; women in silk dresses woven with gold and studded with gems; pages and squires bustling importantly; servants bearing trays; and, best of all, the great King Arthur himself, resting with comfortable dignity on a throne in the center of the hall. The king's beard was almost entirely gray, but his face was unlined, and his eyes were bright. He was chatting with a young knight at his side, but when Sir Kai stepped forward, the king turned his attention to the court and announced, "Let us begin. Kai, you seem to have lined up rather a long day for us."

"Oh, ay, it's all my fault," grumbled Sir Kai.

The king smiled affectionately at his seneschal and said, "Who is first?"

Sir Kai began to lead the various suppliants before the king, and Lynet watched with interest and growing respect as the king questioned each as to his or her request. He was unfailingly courteous, both to noble and to peasant, but he was also firm. To the lady who demanded a knight to avenge the death of her husband, killed in combat, Arthur said, "I am sorry for your loss, my lady, but this court offers only justice, not vengeance." And for none of the lady's wails and moans and tears and vapors would he change his decision. Lynet was at once hopeful and apprehensive, unsure how this wise king would respond to her request. Suddenly, Sir Kai was before her.

"My lady," said Sir Kai to Lynet. "What is your request?"

Startled from her reverie, Lynet leaped to her feet. "Excuse me, your highness," she stammered. "I come on another's behalf, for a beautiful lady."

"Not for your own sake?" asked the king.

"No. At least, not entirely. But I too live at the Castle Per — the Castle Perilous, which is owned by this beautiful lady, and so I too am oppressed. This castle has been besieged for many weeks by a brutal knight who seeks to steal the lady's rich lands."

"And this, ah, beautiful lady has no defender among her own family?" asked the king.

Lynet thought wryly of her indolent Uncle Gringamore. "No, sire. She is an orphan, and she has never married." Sensing that this was her chance, Lynet added, "But she has said that she would marry the knight who delivered her from this oppression."

The effect of this announcement was not what she

47

expected. A low ripple of laughter spread around the court. The king's face was expressionless, but Sir Kai rolled his eyes eloquently. A slender man in an extravagant blouse of orange silk minced forward and bowed deeply. "I wonder," he lisped, "why this lady who is so beautiful and wealthy has not married before."

Lynet felt her anger rising, but she answered politely. "I suppose it is because she has never met someone she cared to marry."

The brightly clad man smirked back at her. "I see. Not because no one has ever asked, then?"

Lynet looked around the room. Though there were many kindly faces among the onlookers, on every face she read disbelief. She remembered the conversation at the Knight's Sabbath, about the lady who must be ugly if her father was giving her away at a tournament, and even remembered Lady Eileen's polite skepticism about the "fairest damsel in England." Frustrated, Lynet turned back to the gaily dressed man. "Why, no," she said. "She received an offer last year, but the man who proposed wore an orange blouse and had little bells on his shoes. He was entirely ridiculous." The court grew suddenly silent, except for a stifled sound from Sir Kai. The man stepped backwards, as if he had been struck, and a tiny tinkling noise came from his feet. Sir Kai grunted again and turned his face, and Lynet added, "Well, you wouldn't have a lady marry someone with atrocious taste, would you?"

The man blinked, then retorted, "I'll have you know that bells are all the rage right now!"

"Oh, I'm so sorry," Lynet replied contritely. "I've never been to court before, and I was not aware that foolishness was in fashion here."

The fashionable man's eyes bulged from his face, but before he could reply, the king interrupted. "Sir Griflet, you forget yourself. You spoke ungraciously to our guest, and you have been justly served." The king turned back to Lynet and, in an apologetic tone, said, "You must forgive my court's reluctance. This is not the first time that a lady has offered marriage in return for some deed, but really very few of my knights are currently seeking brides. It makes it awkward, you see."

Lynet recognized the king's tact and was grateful for it, even as she despaired inwardly. Her only hope of getting a knight to come had been to entice him with her rich and beautiful sister, and now that had failed.

King Arthur continued, "But perhaps one of my knights might undertake to assist your lady, provided that he need not marry her at the end. What is your lady's name, and where is her, ah, castle?"

The question had come. Irrationally, Lynet wished that Roger were with her, willing her to be brave. The thought of the dwarf helped, and she took a deep breath and replied, "Sire, forgive me, but I cannot say."

49

The king's face grew very still. "Cannot? Or will not?"

Lynet would not lie to him. "I will not. Believe me, your highness, I have reasons."

Though King Arthur did not change his expression, Lynet could see anger growing. "You are impudent, my lady," he said softly. "You have come to my court asking one of my knights to risk his life and honor for you, and you are unwilling to risk even your name? Why should I entrust a knight to one who will not trust us?" Lynet felt her hope slipping. The king concluded decidedly. "I will send no knight with you while you remain nameless."

Lynet bowed her head. "Then I must look for help elsewhere," she said.

A new voice broke into the silence that followed Lynet's statement. "Sire, I beg this adventure from you!"

Lynet looked up with relief to see which knight had volunteered, but it was no knight. Instead, the figure who stepped out of the crowd, vaguely familiar, looked like a menial servant. He was tall and seemed strong, but he was shaggy and bearded, and his clothes were grimy and greasy. He carried a tray supporting a bowl. Lynet recognized him as the kitchen servant who had brought dinner to her in Lady Eileen's chambers. "You're joking," she said.

"Beaumains?" asked the king, wonderingly.

"Yes, your highness," the kitchen knave replied. The court burst into laughter, but the servant stood still.

"I'm sorry, Beaumains," King Arthur said. "But to fight a knight is no task for you. I cannot—"

"I am not afraid," the knave replied.

"I am sure you are not," Arthur said soothingly, "but—"

"My liege?" interrupted Sir Kai. "Why not?"

The king looked sharply at Sir Kai and a surprised "Eh?" escaped him.

"You had determined not to send any knight," Sir Kai said. "Surely it would be better to send Beaumains here than to send no one."

"No, it would not!" exploded Lynet. "I would a hundred times rather you sent no one than send your kitchen help! Of all the insults!"

The king glanced at her, and she read sympathy in his eyes, but he only turned to his brother. "Kai? What are you up to?"

Sir Kai's face was impassive. "My lord, I know of no reason that a servant may not prove to be more than he seems. I myself, as your seneschal, am little more than an exalted servant."

"You know better than that, Kai," said Arthur, but he was watching his brother's face intently.

"No, sire," said Sir Kai. "If being a servant makes Beaumains unworthy, than so too am I!"

Lynet interrupted. "I'll tell you what, your highness.

51

Why don't you just let me have Sir Kai. I wouldn't be insulted then."

King Arthur's lips twitched, but Sir Kai answered for him. "Quite impossible, my lady. But perhaps Beaumains is not so bad a choice for you after all. How do you know he is not a skilled fighter?"

Lynet turned and glared at the tall kitchen knave. Suddenly angry, she snatched a walking stick from a nearby courtier and, brandishing it like a sword, snapped, "Let's see."

She lunged forward, swinging the stick. The knave jumped quickly backwards, causing his tray to tilt. The bowl slid back and bounced off the tray, emptying its contents onto his chest. He yelped with surprise as the soup — fish soup, from the looks of it — soaked into his clothes, and he stumbled backwards, sitting down with a thump. In the hush that followed, Lynet strode back across the hall, returned the walking stick to its owner, then looked challengingly at Sir Kai.

Sir Kai almost grinned. "Few of us could stand our ground before such a savage damsel," he said. "Let us hope that when Beaumains faces your knight he is not holding a bowl of soup."

"You'll get this boy killed, Sir Kai," Lynet said softly. Sir Kai shook his head, but he did not answer. Lynet looked at the king. "I will be leaving your court at once, sire. Thank you for your hospitality."

The kitchen knave struggled to his feet and stood, dripping into an aromatic puddle of soup. "And I will go with you, my lady!"

Lynet cast him a look of disdain. "Oh, go clean yourself up, sapskull," she said. Chin high, Lynet walked out of the hall.

IV

QUESTING

Within the hour, Lynet was riding her mare out the main gates of Camelot, having paused only long enough to write a short note to Lady Eileen, thanking her for at least trying to help. At first she was angry, especially at Sir Kai and the presumptuous kitchen knave, but soon her indignation was replaced with gloom. What was she to do now? She had just begun to ponder that prickly question when she heard a drumming of hoofbeats behind her. Turning in her saddle, she recognized the kitchen knave, astride a fine white charger.

"You!" she declared incredulously. "What are you doing here?"

"I have come to deliver thy mistress from the knight who so persecuteth her," the knave replied.

Lynet rolled her eyes heavenward and replied caustically, "I have a better idea. Why don't you deliver

54

me from a dimwitted servant with foolish notions of greatness? And you'd better return that horse to the stables before its owner finds it gone and gives you a switching."

"This horse is my own," he replied.

"Poppycock!" Lynet snapped.

The knave raised his eyebrows. "It is not meet that a lady should use such language."

"No? How about this language? Go home, you cloth-headed ninny! Go back to your dishwater and swill buckets and leave me alone! I don't want your help, and I don't want your company." Lynet sniffed the suddenly pungent air and added, "Especially smelling like that! Have you never taken a bath? Ugh!"

"You may say what you like, my lady, but I shall respond only with courtesy, like unto the model set for all men by the good knight Sir Lancelot," said the young man.

Lynet leaned out from her saddle until her face was close to the kitchen boy's, which was not pleasant, inasmuch as the servant's clothes really did stink. Slowly and clearly, Lynet said, "Kitchen boy, you're stupid and you smell bad. Go away."

Behind his greasy, uncut hair, the kitchen knave set his lips tightly and made no reply. But when Lynet booted her mare into a trot, he urged his horse forward beside her. Angry and frustrated, Lynet nevertheless realized that if this young fool wanted to ride with her, there was little she could do about it. She stopped again. Taking a deep breath, she turned in her saddle. "Look, I can't stop you from being a clodpole. You are as the Lord made you, I suppose. But do you think you could ride downwind?"

"As you wish, my lady," he replied, moving to Lynet's other side.

"And when we come to a stream, perhaps you could have a wash?" she added.

"Yes, my lady. Which direction shall we ride?"

Lynet sighed. "The castle is southwest."

The knave frowned. "But, my lady, this is not southwest. We should be riding that way." He pointed to the left.

Lynet hesitated. All the directional markers that Roger had taught her indicated that she was going the right way, but her confidence was not very high in this area, and muttering her grudging thanks, she turned her horse and let the knave lead the way.

They had not gone far when Lynet again heard the sound of hoofbeats approaching from behind. She turned in her saddle and saw with surprise that it was Sir Kai, fully armored and leading a packhorse. Lashed to the horse's side were two long lances. Beside her, the kitchen knave took a sharp breath and stifled an indignant oath.

"Good day, my lady, my boy," Sir Kai announced cheerfully, reining in beside them.

"What are you doing here?" Lynet asked bluntly.

Sir Kai grinned. "Ah, I was right. A savage damsel indeed. Don't attack me with a walking stick, will you?" He seemed much more pleasant than he had been at court, but his eyes still held a mocking light. "Bedivere can run the court while I'm gone," he added. "I thought I'd best bring you some armor and weapons. After all, if you left the court poorly supplied and got killed, they'd all blame me."

"How thoughtful of you," remarked Lynet sarcastically.

"Ay," Sir Kai said, with a knowing grin. "But that's the sort of chap I am. Here you go, Beaumains. A lovely suit of armor, fit for rescuing damsels and killing all manner of ogres. Try to keep it clean — cleaner than you keep yourself, I mean."

Lynet was not sure if Sir Kai was deliberately provoking the kitchen boy, but whether he intended it or not, he was successful. The boy's eyes flashed, and without a word he dismounted and began to take the armor from the packhorse. While he began awkwardly to put the armor on, Sir Kai sat on his own horse, placidly watching. Lynet edged closer to Sir Kai and whispered urgently, "You'll get him killed, Sir Kai!"

"I think not," he replied calmly.

"No one would bother a wandering servant, but when he puts on that armor, any passing knight may challenge him."

"I hope so. He'll need the practice if he's to defeat this knight that you want rid of."

"You don't need practice to die," Lynet retorted, but Sir Kai only smiled.

At last the kitchen knave had put the armor on. Lowering the helm over his head, he stood tall and loudly declared, "And now, Sir Kai, I challenge thee to mortal combat, for cause of all thy scorn! Thou art a recreant knight!"

"Who, me?" Sir Kai said innocently.

"Since my arrival at court, thou hast spared no pains to heap humiliation upon my person. It was thou who did call me upon scorn 'Beaumains.' And it was thou who set me to menial labors in the kitchens. I challenge thee upon thine honor!" The kitchen knave mounted, smoothly and quickly, despite the heavy armor. From the packhorse, he drew one of the lances. With a shrug, Sir Kai drew the other.

"You're not actually going to joust with this smelly servant boy?" Lynet demanded incredulously. Sir Kai nodded. "Why? What do you have to prove?"

"Didn't you hear, my Savage Damsel?" Sir Kai answered. "I'm a recreant knight. We recreant knights do this sort of thing."

Lynet rolled her eyes helplessly. She could not believe that Sir Kai had actually taken offense at the knave's insults, but she had learned long ago that men were at their most incomprehensible when they thought they were defending their honor.

The two riders took their places at the opposite ends of a field. Sir Kai gave a signal, and they rode toward each other. With a dull thud, then a crash of armor on armor, they came together. Both reeled in their saddles, and both horses reared, but it was Sir Kai who lost his grip and toppled from his horse's back. Lynet stared in amazement at Sir Kai's prone form, but before she could gallop forward to help him, he raised himself stiffly, removed his helm, and grinned at the armed knave above him. "Well hit, boy," he said.

"In future, mayhaps thou'lt think twice before thou scornest a youth!" the kitchen boy said grandly.

"I thought twice before I did it this time, lad," was all Sir Kai said.

Sir Kai left them, having mounted his horse stiffly, and they rode on. Lynet wondered furiously about what she had witnessed. It was impossible that this untrained and unkempt servant should actually be a better warrior than a knight like Sir Kai. Either he had been very lucky or else Sir Kai had allowed himself to be defeated. Of the two choices, luck seemed the most likely explanation, but Lynet could not help feeling that Sir Kai had behaved very mysteriously.

Three hours later they rode out of a stand of trees into a small clearing, empty but for a brightly glowing campfire. "Here indeed is a strange adventure, my lady," said the knave. "A fire burns, yet is there no hand about to have made it. I suggest we dismount and encounter this adventure together. Fear not, for thou art safe with me."

Lynet sighed. The boy must have spent all his time at court listening to minstrels tell courtly tales. "There is no adventure, addlepate. We've ridden into someone's camp, and he's probably watching us from the woods right now, wondering whether you're a madman or just a harmless idiot."

As if to confirm Lynet's assessment, a voice spoke from the bushes at the far end of the clearing, a very welcome voice. "Good Gog, my lady! Is that what Arthur gave you by way of a champion? It's the dim leading the dim!" Roger the dwarf stepped into the clearing.

Lynet smiled with relief, feeling again the stir of amusement that Roger's blunt statements often evoked in her. The knave, however, dismounted quickly and faced Roger. "Speak thou ill of me, as you like, dwarf! I owe thee that. But thou shalt speak no disparagement of a lady in my presence. Retract thy words!"

Lynet dismounted and stepped between the two. Raising her chin and glaring into the kitchen knave's eyes, she said, "Listen to my words, domnoddy. I'll

60

speak slowly. I don't need you to protect me, especially from my friends. I didn't ask you to come. I want you to go away. Has any of that sunk into your brain?"

"Don't waste your time, my lady," recommended Roger. "Nothing short of an arrow could enter that brain."

"Do you know this buffoon, Roger?"

"Oh, ay. I'd recognize his knightlier–than–thou manner of talking anywhere. I'm the one who took him to Camelot. I found him lost in the woods, about to starve. He's not what you'd call a woodsman. Did he tell you his name, by the way?"

"No. Sir Kai called him Beausomething, but I think Sir Kai calls people whatever he feels like: he called me Savage Damsel."

Roger grunted. "Well, he got that right, anyway."

"Beaumains is not my name," interrupted the kitchen knave, removing his helm and setting his various odors free, "but I shall bear that name until I have fulfilled my quest!"

Lynet and Roger looked at each other, then back at the knave. "Right then, Beaumains it is. Maybe it's French for silly ass," Roger said. "Which one of you chose your direction?"

"The silly ass did," Lynet replied. "He said this way was southwest. Don't tell me —"

"You're almost due east of Camelot right now," said Roger. He sighed. "I suppose I'd better ride along, if

61

you're ever going to get home. Why don't we stay here tonight and start in the morning?"

Relieved, Lynet nodded. "Is there a stream nearby where Beaumouse or whatever his name is could wash?"

"He does nif a bit, doesn't he?" agreed the dwarf. "Behind those trees, Beau."

While Beaumains was washing, Lynet briefly told Roger what had happened since they parted, omitting only Terence's part and Lady Eileen's reference to the Seelie Court. Roger listened attentively, and when she was done said, "Do you mean to tell me that... that Beau has been acting as a kitchen boy?" He shook his head slowly. "And nobody at court ever questioned it?"

"Why should they?" asked Lynet.

Roger glanced over his shoulder at the woods where Beaumains had disappeared. "Why, indeed?" he said softly. "He certainly looks the part with that greasy hair over his face. But Kai... perhaps he has some doubts. What did Kai say to you about Beau?"

Lynet was confused, but she said, "Only that he might turn out to be a skilled fighter, but I think that was just a cruel joke." Roger's frown cleared, and he nodded to himself. "What is it, Roger?"

"Just that I understand what Kai's doing now," Roger said. Before Lynet could ask, though, Roger turned on her. "But I still don't know what you were thinking when you refused to tell your name at the gate and at court. What sort of crack-brained notion—?"

"Haven't you figured that out?" Lynet said, stung by his sharp tone. "You know who my father was."

"Ay, Duke Idres of Cornwall. What's that to do with—?"

"You may not know it, but my father once rebelled against Arthur!" Lynet said bluntly.

Roger's mouth dropped open, and he stared at her in consternation. "Is that all?" he gasped. "You mean you thought that Arthur might hold a grudge against you on your father's account?" Lynet nodded, and Roger rolled his eyes heavenward. "You goose! Arthur doesn't care a rap about all that!"

"He doesn't?"

"Listen, girl, have you ever heard who led the rebellion your father was part of?"

"Of course I have. It was King Lot of Orkney," Lynet replied.

"Ay. And you know who King Lot's oldest son is? It's Sir Gawain, Arthur's most loyal knight."

Lynet's eyes widened, as she realized that all her secrecy had been pointless, and that she could have told her name after all and been given a real knight as a champion. Because of her refusal to tell her name, she had ended up with a serving boy instead. "Oh," she said.

Roger must have read her thoughts. "Don't worry, lass. Maybe the Beau will work out better than you think. And speaking of him, I suppose I ought to go check on him—see that he can find his way back to camp."

Lynet smiled wanly, and Roger made his way through the trees where he had told Beaumains he would find the stream. He was gone a long time, but when he reappeared, he brought with him a remarkably different figure. Beaumains's long, greasy hair had been neatly cut over his forehead, and the straggly blond beard had been shaved off. To her amazement, Lynet saw that beneath all that hair, Beaumains was a very handsome young man indeed. His chin was strong, his lips firm, and his eyes a shining blue. Lynet realized that her mouth had dropped open, and she shut it quickly. "You look a bit better, I suppose. Let's hope you smell better, too," she said abruptly.

The next morning Roger took charge and led them southeast. Beaumains argued briefly about their course, but his dispute was clearly only for form's sake. He had no idea himself which way to go, but he resented being led by the dwarf.

An hour later, as they rode along a quiet forest brook, they met their first adventure. A youth, running wildly and gasping for breath, burst out of the brush before their horses. He wore the simple but neatly cut livery of a knight's personal servant, probably a page. "Sir Knight!" he wheezed to Beaumains. "Thank heaven!"

Lynet started to correct the youth's misapprehension, but Beaumains answered quickly, "What is it, young sir?"

"My master, a goodly knight, is in need of help. He is attacked by six thieves, and they'll kill him if no one helps!" The page pointed behind him. "Right through those trees, in an open clearing!"

"I shall aid your master at once!" Beaumains declared. He drew his sword and raised it high over his head.

"Hold up there, Beau," Roger said. "Think a moment. Even if this lad's not setting a trap, you don't need to be charging full front on six enemies."

"Fie on such cowardly caution!" shouted Beaumains. He spurred his white horse forward and charged through the brush. With a muffled oath, Roger rolled his eyes and urged his horse after the vanishing figure.

Lynet followed. When she arrived at the clearing that the page had described, the battle had already begun. At the far end of the meadow, a wounded knight leaned against a tree, holding his sword weakly before him, while Beaumains slashed and shouted at several leaping figures. Two were already sprawled on the grass, and as Lynet watched a third fell before Beaumains's sword. He wheeled his horse to face the last two.

Roger, who sat on his horse a few feet away from Lynet, said suddenly, "Six! The boy said there were six!" Lynet blinked, and then understood. One was missing. "Oh, blast!" Roger said suddenly. "I hate doing this!" He fumbled behind him on his saddle for his sword, managed to pull it out, then booted his horse into a run, across the meadow toward a small stand of trees. Peering into those trees, Lynet saw what Roger had seen: the sixth man, carefully aiming his longbow at Beaumains's back.

Beaumains charged the remaining two that were in the open, and Roger rode yelling at the man in the trees. The dwarf's charge distracted the man enough that his arrow missed Beaumains, and then Roger and his horse were in the trees. Lynet saw the hidden archer reel backwards, struck by the horse's shoulder, just as a low branch swept Roger off his horse's back. He tumbled into a heap, and Lynet kicked her mare into a gallop. When she arrived at the dwarf's form, though, he was sitting up, winded but unhurt. She looked quickly around the meadow. The battle was over. Four men lay dead before Beaumains, and the remaining two had evidently made good their escape, disappearing into the forest.

Lynet dismounted, then stalked furiously across the

field toward Beaumains. "You crack-brained lunatic! Didn't you hear what Roger said? You just about got yourself killed, and Roger too for all your pains! Do you have any idea what almost happened to you?"

"A true knight does not think of death!" Beaumains snapped.

"Especially after he's dead!"

The wounded knight who had been leaning against the tree removed his helm and looked at Beaumains and Lynet. "Pardon me," he said, "but I, um, want to thank you, Sir Knight, for —"

"He's not a knight!" Lynet said. "He's a kitchen boy, dressed up in borrowed armor, playing silly games!"

"But, my lady," the wounded knight protested. "He did save my life."

"I'm very glad that you were saved," Lynet said, "but it was an accident. If this fellow Beaumouth hadn't come on your attackers by surprise and made a few lucky swings, he'd have been killed right away. And if that dwarf hadn't charged when he did, he'd be a kitchen knave with an arrow through his back."

Lynet turned challengly toward Beaumains, but he was silent. Turning on her heel, Lynet strode back to where Roger was gingerly picking himself up. "Have you seen my sword?" asked the dwarf. "I seem to have lost track of it."

"What, again? You really ought to hold on to it tighter," Lynet replied.

"Shut up and help me look," muttered the dwarf. They searched in silence until they found the sword in the tall grass. As Roger put it back on his saddle, he said softly. "My lady?"

"Yes?"

"The Beau *was* brave, you know. Charging six at once like that."

"Brave? Or stupid?"

Roger shrugged. "I've never been sure where brave stopped and stupid began, myself. Give me a boost here, won't you?"

Since Beaumains had led Lynet the wrong direction at first, Roger decided to leave the paths and cut through the forest. His shortcut failed, however. Before they had ridden twenty minutes they came to a river, far too broad and swift for them to cross on horseback. They had to follow along the riverbank until they came to a passable ford. After an hour, Roger's mutterings were growing blisteringly obscene. Lynet had learned several new words.

At last they came to a passable ford, where the river widened somewhat. On the opposite bank were two knights on horseback, both holding lances.

"Hello, good knights!" called Roger. "Can you tell us if this ford is as shallow as it seems?"

"It is a fair crossing," replied one of the knights. "There is no other place for ten miles on either side."

"But you shall not pass," added the other knight.

"I beg your pardon?" replied Roger.

The first knight explained. "It is the custom of this ford that no knight shall cross save he fight with one of us first."

Lynet guided her mare forward. "Well, that's all right, then," she said. "We have no knights here."

"What do you call that?" demanded the second knight, pointing at the armored Beaumains.

"I know it looks like a knight, but don't be deceived by appearances. That's just a kitchen boy in borrowed armor. Not worth your bothering with."

"He holds a lance like a knight," said the first knight.

"Yes, he looks very grand," Lynet said patiently. "But trust me, he'd be much more comfortable with a soup ladle."

The two knights looked at each and seemed to hesitate, but at that moment Beaumains spoke. "I need no lady to speak for me! Sir Knights, I accept your challenge!"

Lynet twisted sharply in her saddle. "Will you shut up?" she hissed. "They were about to let us across."

"I fear no knight alive, except it be the great Sir Lancelot du Lac, who knows no peer in the knightly courtesies and arts!"

The two knights across the river again exchanged glances, then laughed coarsely. "Come on, then, kitchen boy!" said one. "Which of us shall you try?"

"Why both at once, if you be not afeared," Beaumains replied calmly.

"Are you crazy?" Lynet gasped. "Of course you are. I mean, are you determined to kill yourself? These are not peasant thieves with sticks, like the last batch. These are knights! They'll turn you into mincemeat!"

"Beaumince," murmured Roger.

"You're not helping!" Lynet snapped at the dwarf.

"Very well!" shouted the knights. "Both at once! Come on across!"

While Lynet fumed helplessly, Beaumains guided his horse into the river. The water was just up to the pommel of his saddle, and he had to walk slowly so as not to lose his balance in the current. When he reached the middle of the river, he stopped. "Now it is your turn. I have come halfway, and if you be not craven and spineless knights, you will come the rest of the way! Meet me here in the river, cowards!"

At once the two knights spurred their horses into the river. Lynet shook her head and asked, "Do all men act like fools when they're called cowards?"

Roger nodded absently. "Very clever, my Beau," he said softly.

"What do you mean?" Lynet asked.

"Look. In the water, their lances are no good. They can't get enough speed to knock him off the horse, so their spears become awkward. He can fight with his sword. See?"

Sure enough, Beaumains had cast aside his lance and drawn his sword. "It must be just luck," Lynet said. "He couldn't have thought of that himself."

"I certainly didn't think of it," replied Roger.

The battle was short. Beaumains attacked the first figure with his sword, and with his second blow managed to knock him off his horse into the river. The second knight shouted "Brother!" and drew his own sword. He struck and then struck again, but Beaumains parried every blow. At last, Beaumains drove forward and buried his sword's blade in the knight's helm. The knight fell lifeless into the river.

"The other knight hasn't come up yet," Lynet whispered.

"Belike it's hard to swim in armor," Roger said. "Come on, my lady."

When they rose dripping from the water, Beaumains had already removed his helm. His handsome face wore a new expression. His lifted chin indicated a new pride, and his thin-lipped smile spoke of a smug self-satisfaction that irked Lynet to her core.

"Luck!" she said briskly.

Beaumains blinked, then said, "Have ye still no gentle words for me, my lady?"

Something, perhaps pity, stirred in Lynet's heart,

and she said grudgingly, "It was a good idea to meet them in the river." All of Beaumains's smugness returned in a flash, and Lynet added, "Because you needed another bath anyway."

V

The Knight of the Black Woods

Lynet had difficulty going to sleep that night. Whenever she closed her eyes, she saw Beaumains's startled expression and heard again his plaintive question, "Have ye still no gentle words for me, my lady?" At that moment she believed she had seen the real person beneath his assumed self-confidence, his stilted courtly language, his exaggerated respect for Sir Lancelot. She had made little of his moment of triumph, and her scorn had laid him open as no wound could have. But when she had relented, all his ridiculous bravado had returned, and the real human being had retreated again into his borrowed armor.

At last Lynet slept, but it seemed only a minute before a stirring in the night woke her. She sat up in her blankets and looked around. All was still. "Roger?" she hissed. "Did you hear something?" There was no answer, and she looked more closely at the dwarf's bed. Roger was gone.

As before, when she had noticed the dwarf's absence at Camelot, Lynet felt a queer sense of loss. How were they ever to find their way to the Castle Perle without him? Wrapping her cloak around her shoulders, she rose and tiptoed across to Roger's blankets. They were neatly laid back, and a small black opening in the bushes seemed to point the direction he had gone. Without hesitation, Lynet stepped into the forest.

The sky was clear, and the light of a half moon silvered the spaces between trees. Lynet walked slowly in her bare feet, a strange excitement growing inside her. She saw no sign of Roger, but she did not hesitate. At every turning, she knew which way she was to take. After a few minutes, she came to a tiny clearing in the forest. In the center of the clearing was a circle of deep shadow, standing by itself.

As she approached, the dark patch began to expand and change shape. In a moment, it had taken the form of a small man, though a hint of tiny horns amid the tousled hair was distinctly nonhuman. "Hallo, Lynet," said a chuckling voice.

To her surprise, Lynet realized that she was not afraid. "How do you know my name?" she asked calmly.

"Well, at first I wasn't sure. You see in that blue silk dress I took you for a lowly servant girl —" The voice trailed off in an explosion of uncontrollable giggles. Lynet recognized the voice now. It was the same personage who had helped her through the Red Knight's camp on the first night of her quest, the one that Lady Eileen had said was a faery.

"Are you . . . are you a faery?" Lynet asked.

"But of course, my lady. You may call me Robin."

"Good evening, Robin. I want to thank you for helping me through the Red Knight's camp. I'm afraid I was very foolish."

"No more than any other mortal," said the little man with a laugh.

"But I've learned a little since then."

"Not as much as you're going to, Lynet. That's why you're here tonight."

"I beg your pardon?" asked Lynet.

"Can you not feel it? Tonight is a night for enchantments. And you, my lady, whether you know it or not, are going to learn about enchantment." Robin paused, but Lynet did not answer, so he continued. "Do you see the moon? The night of the half face is a night for good magic. Everything good is half light and half dark, you see. Come here, and look at this plant. This is called feverfew, a very useful herb indeed."

Robin sounded like a teacher beginning a class. "Why are you telling me these things?" she asked.

Robin's voice was serious when he answered. "Lynet, my dove, you are intended for much, and

75

much is expected of you. But you have far to go first."

Lynet stepped closer. She felt so wide awake now that she wondered if she was dreaming, but she only said, "What do you do with feverfew?"

For an hour or perhaps two — time seemed elastic in the faery's presence — Robin told her about herbs and spells and charms and much more. Lynet listened intently, drawn by an innate interest as well as by the sense of awe that grew upon her at being tutored by a faery. At last Robin sent her away to get her rest, promised that she would see him again, and disappeared in a twinkling. Bemused, Lynet turned and walked slowly back toward bed.

Not twenty yards from the camp, however, near a small stream, Lynet heard a splash, followed by an unmistakable sigh. She stopped in her tracks and shrank into the shelter of a holly bush. A moment later, she heard another sigh. Cautiously, she peered around the shrubbery, then ducked back into its cover, surprised and embarrassed. Kneeling by a small pool was a tall, angular young man, naked but for a small cloth wrapped around his loins. His shoulders were broad and his arms were muscular, but he was stooped and weary-looking. He had reddish blond hair, cropped short over his face.

It was the young man's face that struck Lynet most forcefully, for even in her brief look she had seen an infinitely deep sadness. His shaded eyes and gaunt cheeks spoke of a sorrow greater than any such young man should have to know. She was about to take one more look when the sound of receding footsteps told her that the young man had left. She forced herself to wait quietly for ten long minutes, until she was sure he would be gone, then she hurried back to camp. Just before she wrapped up in her blankets to return to sleep — if indeed she had not been dreaming this whole time — she remembered why she had left the camp and looked quickly across at Roger's bed. The dwarf was there, sound asleep.

Breakfast the next morning was quiet. Beaumains never talked very much, Lynet was preoccupied with her cloudy memories of her nighttime visit with Robin and of the strange young man by the stream, and even Roger seemed unusually solemn. To make matters worse, breakfast itself was skimpy. On the packhorse that Sir Kai had brought, there had been a neat package of provisions, but traveling was hungry work, and they had finished off all but a few scraps at supper the night before. Lynet did not say anything, but remembering her hunger on the way to Camelot, she was not looking forward to the day's ride.

A few hours later, though, just as the first sharp pangs of hunger began to intrude on her thoughts, Lynet smelled a delicious aroma of seasoned meat over a fire. Riding over a small hill, she saw a slight figure in the neat garb of a squire kneeling over an open spit, turning the brown carcasses of three large rabbits.

"Hello, travelers. Come join my meal," the young man called.

"Blast!" Roger muttered.

"What's wrong, Roger?" asked Lynet.

"I know that fellow. That's Sir Gawain's squire, as uncanny a chap as you'll ever meet."

"Terence?" Lynet asked, with surprise and delight.

"Oh, you've met?" Roger asked.

"Only briefly," Lynet said. "He seemed nice enough at court."

"Ay, he's nice enough. But he sees a sight more than most. If you've any secrets, you may as well tell him now and save yourself the bother." Again, Roger swore softly.

Beaumains reacted most strongly of all to Terence's sudden appearance. Beaumains had been carrying his helm loosely under one arm, but at Roger's words he quickly placed it on his head and lowered the visor over his face. "Woman! Dwarf! I command that thou revealest not my name to this lackey!"

Lynet did not care for being called "Woman!" and she resented still more being ordered about by Beaumains, but before she could retort, Roger said soothingly, "Nay, my lady. Don't fight useless battles."

Turning to Beaumains, Roger said, "Calm down, Beau. We don't know your name, remember?"

Lynet hardly had time to wonder why Beaumains was so afraid of Terence, whom he must have seen hundreds of times at Camelot, when they were upon Terence's camp. "Hello, Squire Terence," Lynet said. "I am very glad to see you."

The squire's eyes laughed. "And so are your two friends, I perceive." Lynet glanced at Roger's glowering face and Beaumains's stiff and silent form, and she giggled. Terence continued. "The chap in armor is Beaumains, I suppose. And your other friend is?"

"This is my good friend Roger, who is guiding us on our journey," Lynet said. She wondered again why no one seemed to recognize Roger, while the dwarf seemed to know everything about everyone in Arthur's court.

Terence nodded a friendly greeting, then gestured behind him. "I don't suppose any of you are hungry, are you? I've just eaten, and I have these three rabbits on the broil."

"Exactly the right number," Lynet said musingly. "What a coincidence! And yes, I am famished. I would be delighted to —"

"We need none of your food, squire!" Beaumains said abruptly.

Lynet, who had already begun to dismount, stopped

and stared. "What are you talking about, flickerwick? We're out of food! You know that."

"I'll not be beholden to this lackey!"

Lynet looked apologetically at Terence. "Don't mind him. I suppose manners are not taught to kitchen knaves." She looked back at Beaumains. "Tell you what. You stay there and pretend to be a knight, and I'll have something to eat. Roger?"

The dwarf's lips twisted in a lopsided smile. "I'd as soon be moving on myself, but that surely smells good." He dismounted.

The rabbit was very good. Lynet was amazed at how tender and succulent the meat was. Terence kindly explained to her which herbs to use for flavor, and she and Roger ate their fill while Beaumains sat aloofly on his horse at the edge of the trees.

When Lynet had eaten enough, she looked up at Terence, who was reclining patiently against a tree. "Squire Terence?"

"Yes, my lady."

"I don't believe that it was a coincidence — your being here with food just when we needed it."

Terence grinned. "Lady Eileen asked me to look in on you and see that you came to no harm. She took quite a fancy to you, you know."

Lynet smiled with pleasure. "Oh, I'm glad. I liked her too. But how did you know where to find us?"

Terence did not answer at first, and Lynet looked

into his eyes. They lit with inner laughter, and one lid dropped in a quick wink. "An old friend told me. He...ah...saw your camp last night when he was gathering herbs in the moonlight."

Lynet smiled back. So this squire knew Robin. She felt suddenly warmed as she realized that she was surrounded by protectors who, for some reason, had chosen to care for her.

"Is your master with you?" asked Roger suddenly.

"Do you know my master, friend Roger?" Terence asked politely.

"Everyone's heard of Sir Gawain," Roger said, his face taut.

Terence looked curiously at Roger, to the dwarf's evident discomfort, but all he said was, "Nay. He's gone off alone on family business."

Trying to distract Terence from his scrutiny of her friend, Lynet said hastily, "Something about his brothers, I think you said back at court?"

Terence looked away from Roger. "Ay, that's it. His youngest brother Gareth made a vow and rode off to fulfill it. Then another of his brothers, Gaheris, went off to find Gareth. Neither one's been heard of since. So Gawain's gone to look."

"Oh," Lynet said suddenly. "I've heard of Gaheris before, but I didn't know he was Gawain's brother. In fact—" Lynet remembered that Roger had served Gaheris and glanced at the dwarf, but Roger shook his head sharply. Lynet hesitated. "In fact, I heard a knight named Sir Dinadan speak of him. He did not seem to think that Gaheris was a very skilled knight."

"He was right," said Terence quietly, "but Gaheris is worth a dozen of Dinadan anyway." Lynet peeked at Roger, who was staring at Terence. The squire stood and stretched, like a cat. "Well, I know you questing ladies have to keep moving. Give this other rabbit to your champion, will you? He may be hungrier later. I'll be off now, but if you don't mind I'll check on you again."

"I'll look forward to it," Lynet said, smiling. And then Terence disappeared into the forest. Lynet looked at Roger, puzzled. "Why didn't Terence know you, Roger, if you used to serve this Gaheris?"

"I was only with him a short time on one of his journeys," the dwarf said.

"But still, you might have been able to tell him something that would help Sir Gawain find him."

Roger shook his head and said nothing.

"Cheery place, this," Roger commented. "Lovely spot for a funeral, I'd think."

They were traveling on a narrow path through the closest, darkest, most ominous-looking forest Lynet had ever seen. The sun was almost completely obscured, and ivy and mistletoe hung low over their heads. Then, as if the natural gloom were not enough, someone had hung long strips of black cloth over some of the branches, and they fluttered gently in the breath of wind that penetrated the trees. Lynet felt the darkness of the path as a chill in her heart.

"What's that?" she asked. On a low branch ahead of them hung something round and dark.

"Looks as though someone's hung a shield up there," Roger said, riding closer. "And there's a lance beside it. Both of them black, of course. Not very imaginative decorations around here. Old Griflet would be appalled."

At the thought of the brightly dressed courtier back at Camelot, Lynet's spirits lifted, and she allowed herself a smile.

"That's the dandy, my lady," Roger said softly. "Don't be cast down by someone's decorations. Any fool can paint a shield black. And look, just past the shield there's a clearing."

It was true; a gap in the trees ahead allowed in a bit more light. "Thank heaven," Lynet muttered.

"Who's there?" came a gruff shout. Lynet took a quick breath, and then they were out of the trees in the clearing, facing a large man in armor as black as coal.

Lynet could only stare, but Beaumains, who had been quiet all day, spoke. "We are travelers seeking a way through this forest."

The man in black smiled with a fierce delight. "A knight!" he exclaimed. "How splendid! Ready your armor for battle!"

Lynet shook off her wonder and said, "Oh for heaven's sake! Why should he? All we want is to pass through."

The Black Knight laughed harshly. "No one passes through here unless they pass through me. If you are a commoner, you pay me a toll. If you are a knight, you fight." He laughed again. "But if you fight, you do not pass. For here you die."

"What a stupid custom!" Lynet protested. "What good can it possibly do you to fight and kill strangers?"

The Black Knight frowned at her, then grinned. He was missing several teeth. "A spirited lady, now! You need taming! Is this knight by your side able to break you to halter as I could?"

Lynet felt suddenly cold inside as she looked into the leering eyes of the huge man, but she forced herself to be calm. "This? This is no knight! This is a kitchen boy who's put on someone else's armor. You'll gain no manly glory by fighting this one. Why don't you let us by and wait for someone more worthy of you?"

The knight stepped closer with an insolent swagger. "A kitchen boy, eh? I ought to thrash him for pretending to be his better. Well, if you have no knight to fight me, then you must pay a toll. I'll take the boy's armor and horse, of course." He paused. "And the lady."

Lynet gasped and edged backwards. From the corner of her eye, she saw Roger's hand steal back and rest on the haft of his sword, but then Beaumains spoke.

"You'll take no toll from us, cowardly knight! Either surrender your arms to me at once, or prepare to fight!"

The knight laughed coarsely. "Ho! A kitchen boy with grand ideas! Very well. I'd as soon kill the child first anyway." Turning toward Lynet he said, "Watch closely. Observe your new master, the Knight of the Black Woods."

Beaumains drew his sword and dismounted, and the battle began. It probably took no more than fifteen minutes, but to Lynet it seemed hours. The Black Knight was a skilled and experienced fighter, but every thrust, every attack that he made was somehow parried. Far faster than his opponent, Beaumains was everywhere, here slipping away from a heavy swing, there flashing a quick blow to an unprotected place on the Black Knight's armor. Some of these blows must have hit home, for soon Lynet saw smears of blood on the black iron. She could hear the Black Knight's labored breathing, but Beaumains was ominously silent. And then, leaping and swinging and turning all in one fluid movement, Beaumains reached through the Black Knight's defenses, rapping his helm so sharply that it fairly flew off his head and across the clearing. Bareheaded now, the Black Knight raised his sword again, refusing to yield. "Who are you?" he managed to gasp, just before Beaumains severed his head from his shoulders.

Lynet turned away from the gory scene, but her heart beat with an odd exhilaration, and she sighed in relief. Roger gently guided his horse between Lynet and the corpse, and he said simply, "Well done, Beau."

Beaumains removed his helm and brushed his fair hair away from his proud face. He looked at Lynet, a hint of challenge in his eyes, and Lynet swallowed. "Beaumains, I . . . thank you. And I'm sorry. I've been a terrible shrew on this journey, I know, but . . . I really didn't mean . . . I didn't want you to be hurt, so I tried to talk people out of fighting you. I was protecting you, I thought, but now . . . now you've protected me. Thank you."

Beaumains bowed to her with the grace of a true courtier, and Lynet's heart beat very fast indeed as she looked at the handsome warrior who had delivered her. Roger turned his back to them both and sat very quietly, looking into the dark woods.

VI

Knights in Many Pretty Colors

It was over an hour before they could resume their
journey, because Beaumains had taken a liking to the
Knight of the Black Woods's armor and had to trade
it for the armor Sir Kai had given him. This took a
while, since the armor was a bit messy and had to be
cleaned. Lynet steadfastly looked the other way.

The delay gave Lynet time to regain her composure.
From the moment that the Black Knight had threatened her until the moment that Beaumains struck off
the knight's head, Lynet's heart had pounded with a
potent mixture of fear and fascination. Her stammered
apology and thanks to Beaumains had sprung from
relief and from an odd shyness. When at last the
three travelers were ready to continue, Lynet was out-
wardly calm, but suspecting that she would be too

self-conscious riding beside her handsome defender, she chose to ride with Roger instead.

"Roger?" she asked quietly, after several minutes of silence.

"Mmm?"

"Beaumains is ... he's quite good with a sword, isn't he?"

Roger glanced at her quizzically, but only said, "One of the best."

The blunt statement took her by surprise. "Really?" she asked, lowering her voice even more.

"Ay. Gawain's better, of course, and Sir Lancelot — wherever he is. Tor could match him, I think, and maybe this Saracen chap, Sir Palomides, who's been in the south recently. Beyond that, I can't think of his equal." He turned in his saddle to look at Beaumains, who was dropping farther and farther behind. "Stay in sight, Beau!" he called. "Don't want you to get lost!"

Lynet pondered the dwarf's words for a minute, then said, "He's more than just a kitchen knave, isn't he?"

Roger hesitated, but said at last, "Seems that way."

Eagerly, Lynet continued, "Do you think he's really a knight? In disguise?"

"What do you think, my lady?"

Lynet nodded quickly. "I think he is. I think he's really a famous knight who wanted to be unrecognized in Arthur's court. That would explain why he hid himself from Squire Terence. He was afraid that Terence would know him if he saw him without his beard and long hair." Lynet allowed herself a small smile. "He *does* look different now," she added dreamily.

Roger ignored this last comment. "Why wouldn't he want to be recognized?"

Lynet paused. "I don't know. Didn't he say something about a quest earlier? Maybe hiding his name is part of it. A vow or something."

"Sounds a bit loony, doesn't it?" Roger's voice was expressionless.

Part of Lynet rather agreed with Roger, but only a small part. "I wouldn't say that," she protested.

Roger sighed softly. "No, I didn't think you would."

"We can't judge him until we understand his motives," Lynet said stiffly.

"Very true," replied Roger. He turned again. "Come *on*, Beau!"

Beaumains had fallen behind again when at last Roger and Lynet rode out of the dark forest. The setting sun ahead of them gave an orange tint to the neat, carefully cultivated fields before them. On a small rise was a well-kept manor house. A man on horseback, evidently returning to the manor from a ride in the fields, stopped and stared at them.

"What ho, travelers!" he called. "You look tired!"

Lynet smiled at his open, friendly greeting. "We are, rather," she said.

"We don't get many wayfarers along here," the man

said, riding closer. "Especially ladies. The forest is a bit much for most of them, I think. Dreadful place, wouldn't you say?"

"Horrible!" Lynet assented.

"You must stay the night with me! Much better than a cold campfire, I should think. Do say yes!"

Lynet hesitated, but Roger nodded slowly. "We thank you, sir," he said.

The man smiled brightly. "Then it's settled. My name is Sir Pertelope. Are you alone?"

"No," Lynet answered. "We've a knight with us. He should be along soon."

At that moment, Beaumains rode out of the forest, and Sir Pertelope's friendly face fell. "Is that your knight?" he asked.

"That's right," replied Lynet.

"Then I am sorry for you, my lady." Lynet remembered suddenly that Beaumains was wearing the Black Knight's armor. She started to explain that her knight was not the Knight of the Black Woods, but Sir Pertelope called to Beaumains first. "Hello, brother."

"Brother?" asked Roger.

"My eldest brother," Sir Pertelope said grimly.

"The Knight of the Black Woods?" Roger asked. Sir Pertelope nodded. Roger took a deep breath and said, "No, friend. That is only your brother's armor.

The knight inside is named Beaumains." Roger's voice was gentle.

Sir Pertelope looked searchingly at the dwarf, then at the approaching Beaumains. At last he said, "I must ask. How did this Beaumains come by my brother's armor?"

"It was a fair fight," Roger said. Sir Pertelope seemed to sag. Roger continued, "I'm sorry, friend, but your brother had threatened the lady."

"I believe it," Sir Pertelope said. "But still, he was my brother." Beaumains joined the group, and Sir Pertelope sat upright in his saddle. "Whence came you by that armor, sirrah?" he demanded, in a different voice.

"But Roger just told you—" began Lynet. Roger laid his hand on her arm and shook his head.

"I took it from a scurrilous knave, a recreant knight of no honor," replied Beaumains.

"That knight was my brother!" declared Sir Pertelope. "For his sake must I do battle!"

"So be it!" replied Beaumains. "Appoint thyself to thine armor, and I shall await thee on yon field."

"Are you both crazy?" Lynet demanded, but Sir Pertelope ignored her. He turned and cantered toward the manor house, and Beaumains turned the other way toward the field he had indicated. Lynet looked at Roger. "They're off their heads!"

Roger shrugged. "I tried to stop it," he said.

"Why does Sir Pertelope want to fight?"

"He doesn't. But it was his brother."

"But his brother was a bounder! A fiend! He was vermin!"

"Ay, and he knows it, too. But it was his brother, you see."

"And what if he gets killed trying to avenge his stinker of a relative? What will that prove?" Roger didn't answer. "Would you risk your life for the sake of a worthless brother?"

Roger did not speak for a long time. At last he nodded. "I already have, my lady. And I may again." Lynet started to speak, but Roger continued, "And before you say anything, let me remind you that you've come all this way for the sake of a sister you don't care so much for either."

A finality in Roger's voice told Lynet that he was through talking, and she decided not to argue, especially since he was right. They sat in silence for several minutes until Sir Pertelope reappeared from the manor, fully armed.

"Gracious, look at that," Lynet exclaimed in surprise. The man's armor, from top to toe, was bright green.

Roger's severe expression lightened, and his lips twitched. "Lovely, isn't it?"

The two knights spurred their mounts and came together with a crash that left the Green Knight on his back in the turf. Then Beaumains dismounted, and they drew their swords. Though Sir Pertelope was not exactly a novice, it was clear even to Lynet's untutored eyes that Beaumains was far more skillful. At last, Beaumains struck the sword from the Green Knight's hand. Sir Pertelope sank on his knees in surrender and bowed his head. "I ask your mercy, sir knight," he managed to gasp.

"Your life shall be spared on one condition!" replied Beaumains. "If this lady grants it."

Lynet gasped. "Me?" Sir Pertelope removed his green helm and turned to her, entreaty in his eyes. "Yes, of course!" Lynet added hastily. "Spare his life!" Startled and pleased by Beaumains's deference to her will, she felt a bit giddy.

"Very well," Beaumains said. "And now you must go to King Arthur, at Camelot, and tell what I have done, that he and Sir Kai may know the mettle of Beaumains."

"Those are two conditions, Beau," Roger pointed out. "You said one."

"No, no," the Green Knight said hastily. "No trouble at all. I've been planning a trip north anyway." He climbed slowly to his feet. "And now, Sir Beaumains, would you honor me by taking your rest in my home this evening?"

CHHO

They spent a very pleasant evening in Sir Pertelope's home, and Lynet was struck again by the incomprehensible behavior of men. Whereas hours before, Sir Pertelope and Beaumains had been seeking to kill each other, now they showed no resentment at all. Sir Pertelope spent most of the evening talking with Roger, who had asked him a question about the cultivated fields around the manor house. Sir Pertelope was clearly a conscientious and knowledgeable landowner, and he was ready to talk about farming as long as anyone would listen. Roger seemed interested, too, and the two had a spirited discussion of land management that lasted long into the night.

The next morning, as they rode, Lynet teased Roger about his unexpected interest in coombs and hedgerows and such matters. Roger just grinned and said, "Nothing more lovely than a field of wheat, ready to harvest."

"Huh, maybe to you and that green fellow back there, but you two left Beaumains and me completely out of the conversation," Lynet said.

"I've complete faith in your ability to horn into any conversation you want, my lady. And as for Beaumains, he has no conversation. Our Beau doesn't have two thoughts in his head to rub together to make a fire with. All he cares about is fighting."

Offended, Lynet lifted her chin. "That was very unkind of you, Roger. Think what we owe Beaumains!"

"I do, my lady. Every minute of every day." Roger booted his horse ahead. Angry, Lynet let him go and fell back to ride beside Beaumains. Once or twice she spoke, but Beaumains answered only with monosyllables, and Lynet resigned herself to boredom.

Two hours later, they rode up to a shallow river, where Roger sat on his horse talking with a knight. The knight wore dusty and faded armor of a distinctly pink hue, minus the helm and breastplate, which had been laid aside for comfort's sake. The knight sprawled under a tree holding a long lance, to which was tied a fishing line. He was a picture of relaxed contentment.

When Lynet and Beaumains rode up, though, his demeanor changed. As soon as he saw Beaumains, he scrambled to his feet and gasped, "Percy! What are you doing this far south?"

"My name," Beaumains said loudly, "is not Percy."

"You're not Sir Percard, the Knight of the Black Woods?" the man in pink asked.

"I am not."

He relaxed. "Thank heavens. For a minute there, I thought you were my brother. Hate to say anything bad about family, you know, but old Percy's a bit of a rotter. Happy to meet *you*, though." Lynet stiffened at the revelation that this young knight was another brother of the Black Knight's.

"Mayhaps you will be less happy, sir, when I in-form you that I have killed your villainous brother," Beaumains said rigidly.

The man in pink nodded sagely. "That would be how you got his armor."

Beaumains lifted his chin. "If you seek vengeance, I am at your service."

The man pursed his lips, then shook his head. "No, thank you. As I said, Percy was a stinker. He probably deserved everything he got."

Lynet could not help glancing at Roger, who was grinning back at her. This easygoing knight evidently had a different approach to family loyalty than his green-clad brother did.

"Are you so craven, indeed?" Beaumains demanded, evidently much shocked.

"Leave it be, Beau," interjected Roger. "It's not cowardly to turn down an unnecessary fight."

"That's my view exactly, friend," the strange knight said, smiling. "In fact, not so long ago, I saw Sir Lancelot himself turn down a fight."

"You lie!" Beaumains exclaimed wrathfully. "Never has that great knight so demeaned himself."

The young knight was taken back by Beaumains's vehemence, but he replied calmly. "Nothing demeaning about it. He passed through here, oh months ago, and I was feeling my oats. So, I asked if he'd like to joust with me. He said there was nothing he wanted to do less, that he was tired of fighting. So, we shared a meal and—"

"I said you lie, knave!" shouted Beaumains, drawing his sword. "And for telling such craven falsehoods, you must die!"

The knight looked plaintively at Roger. "What's wrong with this fellow?"

"He was dropped on his head when he was a baby," answered Roger.

"Really?" the man said, diverted. "That happened to another brother of mine. He wears a sort of blue armor. Poor chap never quite got over the knock. Dim, we used to call him."

"You called your own brother Dim?" Roger asked.

"Just a friendly name. And he never minded, because we told him that 'Dim' was another word for 'Courageous.'"

"He didn't believe that, did he?"

"I told you. Dropped right on the noggin, he was." Roger and the knight chuckled together now, and Lynet felt the tension ease.

"Hast thou not heard my challenge?" Beaumains demanded of the strange knight.

Roger ignored him and asked, "You say this dim, ah, courageous brother of yours wears blue?"

The knight nodded. "Yes, and I've another brother who wears green. It was mother's idea. She liked things colorful. I believe old Percy only wore black because he knew she'd hate it. Nasty fellow, Percy."

Roger smiled, but his brow furrowed. "But, forgive me," he asked politely, "what color are you supposed to be?"

The knight glanced ruefully at his armor. "Mother wanted me to be 'The Crimson Knight,' but it's gone a bit pink in the sun, hasn't it? I really should touch it up. Embarrassing to be 'The Pink Knight.'"

Her sense of humor stirred, Lynet interrupted. "It's really quite a lovely shade of rose. How about 'The Knight of the Rose'?"

Roger and the knight chuckled, and the knight stepped toward Lynet in greeting. "Or you could call me Sir Perimones, my lady. It's my name."

Before Sir Perimones reached Lynet, though, Beaumains stepped between them. "Draw thy sword, foul recreant!" he demanded, "for cause of thy cowardice and thy lies about Sir Lancelot." He took a menacing step forward. "I shall not rest until thou art cleaved in twain."

Sir Perimones frowned and glanced at Roger. "Is that right? 'Cleaved'?"

"I thought it was 'clove,'" Roger said pensively.

"Oh, I don't fancy that," Sir Perimones protested. "It sounds like part of a recipe. Is it 'cleaven,' maybe?"

"Look," Roger said. "You say 'cloven,' don't you? Like 'cloven hoof'? So it must be 'clove.'"

Lynet looked at Beaumains, standing awkwardly to one side, and she felt almost sorry for him. Clearly no one had ever told him what to do when a challenge was ignored.

"Hold on," the knight said suddenly, "what about 'cleft'?"

Roger nodded dubiously. "Maybe. What do you think of 'clave'?"

Beaumains had had enough. He pushed roughly in front of Roger and with one heavy, gauntleted hand struck Sir Perimones across the face. Lynet gasped, and Roger sighed.

"Oh, blow it all," Sir Perimones said, rubbing his cheek. "All right, I'll fight. Just let me armor up." He fastened on his breastplate, put on his helm, and then carefully propped his fishing lance in the crook of a tree. "Watch this for me, will you?" he said to Roger. Roger nodded, and the knight drew his sword.

Beaumains lunged forward, but Sir Perimones parried his blow and stepped back. Beaumains lunged again, and again the knight slipped aside. Roger chuckled suddenly.

"Why are you laughing?" Lynet asked. "This is all so stupid."

"Watch Pink, there. He's not fighting at all."

"What?"

"It's a schoolboy's game. You don't try to hit your opponent, you just defend yourself and wait. Of course he can't win the fight that way, but so long as he doesn't attack, Beau can't win either. It's how...how Sir Gaheris almost always fights. You may as well get comfortable. This'll take a while."

Roger was right. The two knights danced around and around, with Beaumains charging and Sir Perimones retreating. At last Beaumains began to show his frustration and call out insults. "Fight like a man, thou dog!" he gasped between breaths. "Ne'er have I faced so craven a knight!"

"Can't hit me, can you?" Sir Perimones replied. "Nyah nyah!"

"You fight as a woman!"

"Can't say I agree with him there," Roger commented to Lynet. "My belief is that women are more bloodthirsty than men."

"Poppycock!" Lynet snapped. "You don't see us trotting around in armor picking fights."

"No, but that's because women are too vain to wear armor. They couldn't show off their maidenly figures."

"Stuff!" replied Lynet. "Men are just as vain as women. Think of those cute little tights that courtiers mince around in! Imagine if a woman wore something like that!" Roger smiled, and Lynet said, "Well?"

"I'm imagining! I'm imagining!"

"Oh, shut up," Lynet said, stifling a giggle.

Beaumains and the stranger continued their defensive dance for another quarter of an hour, and Lynet began to get bored. Glancing around the field, she noticed the knight's fishing lance jerking and bobbing. "Roger! He's got a bite!"

The lance lurched toward the river. "Grab it!" Roger called.

Lynet reached it first, clutching it just before it went into the drink. "What do I do?"

"Pull it out!" commanded Roger.

Lynet jerked up with all her strength, and a large speckled fish came flying out of the river. It flew in a smooth arc over Lynet's head and, as if it had been aimed, smacked Beaumains in the helm. He whirled about quickly, and while the twisting trout was still in the air, sliced it neatly in half with his sword.

"Look what you've done, deuce it!" Sir Perimones exclaimed, irate. "You've gone and clefted my dinner!"

"I beg your... I'm terribly... I didn't see what it was," stammered Beaumains.

"That makes no odds!" Sir Perimones snapped. "It's not very knightly to go fighting a fish, now, is it? I can tell you that Sir Lancelot never had single combat with a trout."

"I said I was sorry!" Beaumains said.

"Look here," interposed Roger, stepping between the two knights. "Suppose we stop all this at once. Beaumains, you've already apologized for clooving this fish. Now, if Sir Perimones will agree that Sir Lancelot never did anything cowardly in his life, we can make peace."

"Oh, ay, I'll agree to that," Sir Perimones said amiably.

For a long moment, Beaumains considered Roger's proposal, then he nodded reluctantly. "Very well, sir knight." Lynet let out her breath in a long sigh of relief. Stiffly, Beaumains sheathed his sword and re-mounted. "Let us be off," he said imperiously.

"Sorry about your fish, O Knight of the Rose," Roger said, grinning. He glanced over his shoulder. "Other direction, Beau!"

The three travelers continued along cultivated fields and neat hedgerows until the sun's light began to fade and weaken toward evening. They passed tidy cottages and one or two small villages, but saw no more knights or noble landlords until they topped a long, wide hill and looked down into a pleasant valley. There they saw every sign of knights—flags and pennants, horses and armor, squires and pages—though knights themselves were conspicuously absent. Two rows of blue tents stood at the center of the valley, framing a long, straight path between them.

"Looks as if someone's set up a tournament," Roger commented. "There's the jousting lane there between the tents."

Lynet's memory stirred. "I think I've heard of this. Sir Persant of something or other sets up a tournament ground hereabouts, and passing knights all get to joust with him. If this is the place, then we're only half a day or so from home."

"Well, that's good, anyway," Roger commented. "But I wonder if we could give the place a miss. I'd rather not give Beau a chance to pick another fight."

"Beaumains doesn't pick fights," Lynet replied haughtily.

Roger stared at her with patent astonishment. "Doesn't he, then?"

"No. His fights were forced on him by others."

"Even the fight with the Pink Knight?"

Lynet was less comfortable explaining away this last battle, but she said, "He thought the other knight had insulted Sir Lancelot." It sounded lame even to her own ears, and she was grateful that Roger did not reply. The dwarf contented himself with a brief, sour glance.

Beaumains, who had been lagging behind again, rode up. "It is a noble place," Beaumains said. "A goodly tilting yard. Let us go forth and see what adventure may befall us."

Roger shrugged and wordlessly led the way down the hill to the blue tents of the encampment. As they approached, several servants and a few ladies stopped to gaze at them. A young page dashed into the largest of the tents, and a moment later a large knight in blue armor appeared at the door. "Welcome, good knight!" the blue knight roared genially.

"Blue armor, hey?" muttered Roger.

"I bid you welcome!" the large knight bellowed again. "But I've already said that, haven't I? Bless my soul!" He laughed uproariously, as if he had made a fine joke. Lynet could not help glancing at Roger, who was grinning broadly. The knight continued, "I am Sir Persant of Indigo!" He paused, and in a conspiratorial voice that probably could have been heard for only a hundred yards, added, "That's why I wear indigo armor, you know!" Then he laughed again.

Lynet looked at Roger. "You don't think this is the one that—"

"A very colorful family, indeed," Roger said.

They rode up to Sir Persant, who beamed at them. "You look a fine fellow!" he exclaimed to Beaumains. "As dim a knight as I've ever seen!"

Beaumains frowned. "What meanest thou by 'dim,' sir knight?"

"Why, full of courage, of course," the knight replied.

Beaumains still looked puzzled, but Roger quickly replied, "You're too kind, Sir Persant. I'm sure you are every bit as dim as Sir Beaumains here."

Sir Persant roared with laughter. "Well spoken, master dwarf! Mayhaps if this knight, Sir Bowman, will oblige me—"

"Beaumains," interposed Roger.

"Of course! Sir Beaumains! If Sir Bowman will oblige me, we'll soon see which knight is the dimmest!"

"Impossible! Two farthings to a ha'penny," murmured Roger. Lynet was indignant at the way Roger was making game of Beaumains, but she could not speak for fear of giggling.

"A joust, then!" shouted Sir Persant, "if it belikes you, Sir Bowman."

"I shall refuse no challenge!" Beaumains said.

"'Tis dimly said!" Sir Persant announced approvingly, and the two knights began making ready for their joust.

"You're horrible!" Lynet gasped to Roger when the knights were out of earshot. "Oh, it's too cruel of you! You've got to let this poor blue knight know what 'dim' really means!"

"What, and contradict his brothers? Nay, lass."

"What did you call me?"

"I beg your pardon, my lady. I come from the north, where people use 'lass' as a sign of respect."

"Do they?" Lynet asked suspiciously, but Roger's face was bland and innocent. Lynet changed the subject. "What about this joust? Do you think Beaumains is in any danger?"

Roger shook his head decisively. "Against this buffoon? Nay."

But Roger was wrong. While Beaumains unhorsed

Sir Persant easily in the jousting, the two knights were much more evenly matched when they began to spar with swords. At last Beaumains disarmed Sir Persant with a very tricky bit of swordsmanship, and the blue knight yielded good-naturedly, but as he left the field, Beaumains stumbled and fell.

Lynet was at his side in a moment. She raised his visor and saw with shock that his face was pale. Only then did she notice the blood that smeared his left shoulder. "Roger!" she screamed.

"Here, lass!" came the dwarf's reassuring voice. "Let me loosen his armor."

Roger swiftly removed Beaumains's breastplate, revealing a deep cut in the shoulder, still ebbing blood. Lynet felt faint, but she shook herself and took charge, pressing her own scarf over the open wound and calling to some of Sir Persant's servants who were standing nearby gawking. "You! And you! Carry Sir Beaumains to a bed, and gently now!"

While the men gathered the weakly protesting Beaumains in their arms, Lynet looked at Roger. "Will he...do you think...?"

"Die? Nay, my lady. But he's not going anywhere for a while. Come on, then. Courage! Let's go see him comfortable now."

VII

ROGER'S JOURNEY

It was a long night for Lynet. When she saw Beaumains's gory wound, her senses reeled, and for the first time in her life, she understood how a person might faint. But she had never had any patience with such missish behavior, so by sheer will, she followed the servants who carried Beaumains to a nearby tent. Then, while they stood gaping and clucking at the prostrate figure, she cleaned and bandaged the cut in his shoulder herself. Beaumains protested feebly, muttering that it was nothing, but Lynet ignored him.

She had no sooner finished binding the wound when she began to have visitors. First, Sir Persant came, making thoughtless comments in an absurd whisper, first saying he was sure Beaumains would be fine by tomorrow, then adding that it was a shame for such a fine knight to be slain so young. To make matters worse, Sir Persant brought with him his daughter Violet, a wispy damsel of about Lynet's age who sobbed and moaned and carried on as if it were her father who was wounded instead of a stranger. Lynet managed to get rid of them only to be beset by Sir Persant's private physician, who came to bleed Beaumains and to prescribe a depressing diet of gruel and goat's milk "if the knight should ever wake up." Beaumains seemed much weaker after the treatment, and Lynet resolved to keep the leech away from him in the future.

The only useful visit was from Roger, who brought her a plate of food, then stayed with her through the rest of the night, while Beaumains dozed and moaned and once asked in a small voice for his mother. Lynet was touched, but Roger answered grimly, "She's not here, lad. You'd best get used to that." Lynet wondered at the harshness of Roger's tone, but it worked. Beaumains relaxed and went back to sleep.

When morning came, Beaumains seemed to be sleeping more deeply than he had all night. Lynet left Roger to watch the patient and slipped out of the tent into the freshness of the dawn. No one else in camp was stirring, and she was able to set off for the fields unobserved. For some hours she had been remembering all that Robin had taught her about the healing herbs, especially feverfew and woundwort, and she had resolved to gather these and take Beaumains's care entirely into her own hands.

She had just reached an uncultivated area where wildflowers and grasses grew in profusion and was casting around for plants she recognized when a chuckling voice behind her said, "Looking for these, my lady?"

Lynet turned quickly to find Robin holding out a small basket filled with freshly cut herbs and bark. Lynet smiled with genuine pleasure. "Hello, Robin. Are those for me?"

"For you? Why, my lady! Have you been fighting, too? Really, Lady Lynet, it's not at all the thing for—"

Lynet rolled her eyes. "I mean, are they for me to use on Beaumains?"

Robin grinned and nodded. "Here, let me show you what I've gathered." For the next hour, Robin carefully explained each herb he had provided, how it was to be used, and what benefit it bestowed. Lynet listened attentively, and when at last Robin finished, she was confident that she could undertake Beaumains's treatment without further help.

"Off you go then," Robin said at last. "Patch the chap up as quickly as you can."

"How long do you think until he's completely recovered?"

"Oh, dear lady, you can't wait that long!" Robin

exclaimed. "Your sister's just about to give in and marry the Knight of the Red Lands!"

"What? She wouldn't!"

Robin's eyes danced. "Of course not. Having such a high view of love and marriage, she'd never stoop to marry a rotter, now, would she?"

Lynet moaned softly. Lyonesse had always viewed marriage as a social step, a chance to latch on to someone else's fame and fortune. "But how do you know she's about to give in?" Lynet asked.

"I dropped in to visit your castle last night." Robin smiled at her and added, "No, she didn't see me. Belike your sister's not very observant."

"But Beaumains won't be able to fight for weeks!" Lynet said.

"Tell him to get well soon, why don't you?" Robin said cheerfully. Then he disappeared into the long grass.

Back at camp, Lynet found Roger unsuccessfully trying to dissuade a groggy Beaumains from getting out of bed and putting on his armor. Lynet took charge at once. "No, Beaumains. You will *not* get out of bed yet," she said, gently but firmly leading him back to his cot. "For heaven's sake, Roger, what were you thinking?" she asked over her shoulder.

"*I* couldn't stop him!" Roger retorted, affronted. "What was I to do? Tie his ankles together?"

"If necessary," said Lynet shortly, turning back to

Beaumains. "You lie down for now. I have some herbs here that will make you feel better, but you have to rest while I prepare them."

Beaumains lay docilely, even gratefully, back on the bed. The exertion of standing had clearly been too much for him. "Mother used to know about herbs," he murmured, half to himself. Lynet watched him tenderly as he closed his eyes. He really was not very old, after all. She longed to stroke his hair and sing him to sleep, but she had medicines to brew.

"How do you know about herbs?" asked Roger, as they left the tent.

"Oh, just picked it up here and there," Lynet replied vaguely. Roger was clearly dissatisfied, but he did not press her. Lynet changed the subject. "We need to get Beaumains well quickly, too."

"Why the rush?"

"My sister is about to...I'm afraid my sister will give up waiting for us and surrender to the Red Knight. If we could get word to her that we were on our way, then she would wait. Do you think you could deliver a message?"

"With this Red Lands fellow camped outside her gate?" Roger said. "Sounds simple enough. I'll just bash my way through his camp, drop off a letter, then bash my way back, shall I? As Sir Persant would say, I can be just as dim as Beaumains."

Lynet whirled around and glared at the dwarf.

"Stop it," she snapped. "Stop making fun of him! He has borne all your criticism like a true knight and gentleman, and he has proven himself brave and noble. Now that he's weak and wounded, leave him alone!"

"All *my* criticism?" Roger retorted. "I haven't called him the half of what you've called him! Have I called him 'kitchen boy'?"

Lynet took a deep breath. "You're right. I did call him names when we first met, and I regret every one of them now. As I told you already, I'm convinced that he is *not* just a kitchen boy!"

"Are you then?" said Roger with a snort. "Well, as soon as I'm convinced that the Beau isn't dim, I'll regret my words, too."

"You know what I think? I think you're jealous!" Roger stared at her, speechless, and she continued, "You can't fight, can't hunt, can't do anything manly, and he can, so you're jealous!"

Lynet didn't believe any of that, of course, but in her anger, she aimed her words toward the most likely sore spot, and not toward the truth. It worked. Roger closed his mouth and set his lips, then turned sharply away from Lynet. It is hard for dwarfs to stride firmly, their legs being so short, but Roger managed to walk away with dignity. Lynet watched him go, suppressed an impulse to call out an apology, and went off to brew her potions.

For three days, Lynet stayed with Beaumains, treating his wound with soothing salves and giving him potions to ease his fever and help him sleep. By the second day, his appetite had returned. Lynet rejected Sir Persant's physician's diet and gave Beaumains whatever he felt like eating. By the third day, he was much improved. He was still weak and his left shoulder still very painful, but he was able to sit up and talk and even receive long visits from the silly Sir Persant and his equally empty-headed daughter. Lynet was well satisfied with the results of her care.

Lynet's only concerns were her nagging worry about Lyonesse and her frustration with Roger. The dwarf had withdrawn from her. He spoke to her seldom, and when he did, it was politely, even punctiliously. Lynet discovered that without Roger to talk to, she ended up talking to no one at all. Then, on the fourth dull day after Beaumains had received his wound, as Lynet walked toward the camp with fresh herbs from the fields, she saw Roger step into Beaumains's tent, then step quickly back out.

Roger saw her too. "Don't go in there, my lady!" he said sharply.

"For heaven's sake, why not?"

"It's . . . it's not a good place . . . he's dressing."

"Well, he ought to be in bed," Lynet said with a scowl. "He's been up all morning, and he needs rest."

"Oh, he's in bed all right," Roger said. "But he doesn't need any help right now."

"I thought you said he was dressing," Lynet said suspiciously.

"I lie a lot. Never trust a dwarf. But Beau's resting comfortably now. He doesn't need you."

"I'll just put some more salve on his wound, then leave him alone," Lynet said, stepping forward.

Roger barred her way. "No, Lady Lynet," he said loudly. "I think that the Beau is ALREADY ASLEEP. Why don't you leave him alone for now?"

"If you haven't wakened him with your caterwauling, I certainly won't disturb him," Lynet said with a frown. She heard a rustling inside the tent. "There, see? He's awake."

Roger licked his lips, then said, "Oh, very well, go on in. But I would have thought that you'd be more concerned about your horse."

"My mare? What's wrong with her?"

"Didn't Sir Persant's grooms tell you? She hit her leg on a branch. It may be broken, they say."

"Broken!" Lynet gasped, dropping her basket of herbs. "No one's told me a thing! Is she still in the paddock?"

Lynet hurried to the area set aside for the camp's horses, where she found her mare perfectly well. None of the grooms knew of any injury to the mare, and with a puzzled frown she returned to the camp. After a quick peek at Beaumains, who was sleeping peacefully, she began to look for Roger. After two hours of fruitless searching, she asked Sir Persant, who replied, "Oh, your dwarf! Ay, I forgot to tell you. He said he was off to take a message to your sister. Good fellow, that dwarf!"

Roger was gone for two weeks, a century to Lynet. She hardly slept at all, and when she did collapse into fitful slumber, she dreamed of Roger's body, hacked and bloodied by the Red Knight's sword, lying at the gates of the Castle Perle. During the day she devoted herself to Beaumains, watching over his wound and keeping him from overexerting himself, but Beaumains was young and strong, and he healed quickly. Soon there was little Lynet could do, and she was content to let Sir Persant and the insipid, giggling Violet entertain her patient while she paced in her tent or tramped across the fields, trying to think of anything but of what might have happened to the dwarf.

But at dinner one night, while Beaumains and his host were enjoying a roast boar, Violet was eating sweetmeats, and Lynet was wishing herself elsewhere, a well-remembered voice at her elbow said, "Never seen you with no appetite, my lady. Figured you'd still be hungry on your deathbed."

It was Roger, dusty and travel-stained, but unhurt. Lynet felt almost faint with relief and managed to whisper, "You're back."

"Ah, but you're as quick-witted as ever," Roger said. "Ay, I'm back."

Lynet leaned close to the dwarf. "You cretin!" she hissed. "You absolutely cloth-headed domnoddy! You witless block! You sap-skulled idiot! You ought to be taken out and beaten with rods! Do you have any idea how foolish this errand of yours was?"

"No, why don't you tell me?" Roger retorted. Lynet glared at him, panting after her outburst, and Roger grinned. "Missed me, did you, lass? Your sister says that she *was* thinking of surrendering to the red chap — odd how you knew that — but she'll be happy to wait now and give Beaumains his chance. If you don't want that plate of boar, can I have it?"

"Get your own," Lynet replied, starting hungrily on the food before her.

Roger turned to Beaumains. "I've a message for you, Beau."

Beaumains, who had not noticed Roger's return but who showed no surprise or interest, said, "For me?"

"Ay. The Knight of the Red Lands says to tell you to bring your burial clothes when you come to fight him. He says he doesn't care who you are, even if you're Gawain or Lancelot himself, he'll chop you to pieces and hang you from a tree." Roger paused, musing, "I don't see that, myself. I mean, will he hang you up first and then chop? Because once you're chopped up, it'll be hard to hang—"

"Shut up, Roger," Lynet said through a mouthful of food.

"Maybe he'll just hang the bigger pieces."

"Roger," Lynet said dangerously. The dwarf grinned at her, but was silent.

"The Knight of the Red Lands!" exclaimed Sir Persant. "Is that who you mean to fight? Gracious, man! He's a monster! He's a head taller than any other man, and he has seven times the strength of a normal knight! I call him the dimmest knight now living! You mustn't fight him, I tell you!"

Beaumains started to speak, but Roger interrupted. "You know this Red Lands fellow, do you? Not a relative of yours, by any chance?" Sir Persant emphatically denied this, and Roger glanced at Lynet. "I was just curious," he explained, "what with all the colorful armor in the family."

Sir Persant, meanwhile, had renewed his entreaty for Beaumains not to fight Red Lands.

Beaumains stood, his lips firm and his chin high. "It is for that fight alone that I have come this great distance, and I will not show craven, whatsomever say ye! This knight's scorn for the great Sir Lancelot only doubles my resolve to defeat such a recreant! We leave on the morrow!"

"Tomorrow?" gasped Lynet. "You're not well enough yet!"

"I will not take thy womanish counsels!" Beaumains declared grandly. "Dwarf, prepare for the journey!"

"Now see what you've done," Lynet moaned to Roger, who was ignoring Beaumains and helping himself to some pork. "He'll get himself killed!"

"Sorry," Roger said. "You have to admit, though. He's very brave."

"Not brave," Lynet muttered. "Dim!"

Roger grinned again.

Lynet had to wait until the others had gone to bed before she could get Roger's story from him. They sat alone by a fire, a little apart from the tents, and Roger stretched his toes toward the flames and began, "It was easy enough traveling, at first—"

"Wait half a moment," Lynet interrupted. "Why did you leave, anyway?"

"You asked me to, didn't you?" Roger replied warily.

"Yes, but you said it was crazy, and you were right!"

"I suppose I was tired of waiting around here, doing nothing. Are you going to let me tell my tale?" Lynet scowled at him, but she folded her hands demurely and waited. "Thank you," Roger said, with a nod. "I knew the right direction, of course, so in a few hours I knew I was near your castle. I didn't really have a plan for how I was to get through this Red Lands fellow's camp, but I thought if I saw it one might come to me."

"Optimistic, weren't you?"

"Well, no, but I couldn't think of anything else. Luckily, I didn't need a plan."

"How did you get through, then?"

Roger paused and licked his lips. Incongruously, he asked, "Have you ever heard of the Other World, Lynet? The world of the faeries?" Lynet looked at him quickly and nodded. "Ay, I thought you might have. Well, I've never had any doings with it myself, but I've some family members who've meddled with such things. Hasn't improved them any, as far as I can see. Anyway, that's one reason I've been a bit leery of this Squire Terence. If anyone's an Other Worlder, he is."

"Did you meet Squire Terence?" Lynet asked, beginning to understand.

"Ay. I was almost to your castle when I came on him, sitting atop a horse as cool as you please, waiting for me. Seemed to know what I was doing, where I was going, everything he needed to know. Uncanny, I call it. He took me to a shed in the woods, where we left our horses, then led me to a spot where we could see the Red Knight's camp and your castle on the other side.

"Well, we waited there a bit, watching the camp from the trees. Once a huge old wolf found us, looked right at me and licked its lips, but Terence told it to take itself off, and off it went." Roger shook his head wonderingly. "Finally at dusk, Terence said it was time—something about its being a time for good magic when it was halfway between light and dark—and we walked out of the forest as bold as you please."

Roger paused. "You may not believe this, but it's so. We walked right through that camp, not three feet from a whole pack of soldiers. They were close enough to smell, and they weren't any bouquet of flowers, let me tell you. We walked right up the hill to your gate, where the portcullis lifted and let me in. I walked inside, and Terence was gone. Like I say, I wouldn't have believed it myself—"

"I believe you," Lynet said quietly. They sat in thoughtful silence for a moment. Then Lynet asked, "What happened then?"

"Well, I found your sister. I say, Lynet, are you sure you two are related?"

"She's much prettier than I am, I know—"

Roger snorted. "Not in any way that matters!"

Lynet felt herself blushing and was glad of the darkness. "What happened?" she asked.

"I told her the whole story, how you'd risked your life to bring back a knight to help her, and all she could do was wish you'd brought Gawain or Lancelot or somebody really famous. She even asked if you could go back and try again for a better knight."

Lynet sighed. "Sounds like Lyonesse. What did you say?"

Roger grinned sheepishly. "I told her that those knights had very high standards and that they wouldn't rescue her unless she were prettier."

"You didn't!" Lynet gasped. "What did she do?"

"She changed color, a bit like the Pink Knight, and gave me a nasty look. You know," he added pensively, "I don't think she likes me above half."

Lynet clucked in mock sympathy. "You couldn't have said anything more likely to get under her skin."

"Well, that's what I thought, too," Roger replied, gratified. "Anyway, I told her what you thought, that Beaumains is really some famous knight in disguise. It was enough to get her interested. She said that if that's true, then she'll let him rescue her."

"She didn't say that!" Lynet exclaimed. "Even Lyonesse—"

"S'truth!" said Roger. "She told me to come on back and give you her permission to bring him on. Then she sent me out."

"In the dark? Didn't she even let you stay the night?"

"She didn't mention it, and to say truth I wasn't in any hurry to stay myself. I thought maybe that magic would still be working, and I could slip back through the camp as easily as I did the first time."

"Did you?"

Roger shook his head. "If I had, I'd have been here two weeks ago. No, I was captured almost before I'd gone ten yards."

"I wonder why Terence helped you in, then didn't help you out," Lynet said, frowning.

"I thought about that a good bit myself," Roger admitted. "But I don't know. I can't even explain why the Other Worlders do what they do; I'll never figure out why they don't do what they don't." He paused. "Does that make sense?"

"No. So you were held captive for two weeks."

"Ay. Old Red Lands heard that I'd been taken coming out of the castle, and he brought me in to ask what they were thinking inside. I was to be an informer, you see. So I told him that Lyonesse was secretly in love with him and talked about him all the time—"

"Roger!"

"I think I told you once: I lie a lot. Anyway, it worked. He kept me alive so that every day or so he could bring me in and I could tell him all the wonderful things that your sister says about him. He'd sit and chuckle and wipe his nose on his hand and scratch himself, and I'd tell him how she thought he was the picture of the knightly courtier and so on."

Lynet made a face. "Sounds horrible. How did you get away?"

"Well, finally, I couldn't take it anymore, and I

figured he'd kill me when my imagination ran out anyway, so when he brought me in, I told him I'd been lying to him, that I was really from Camelot, and that a great knight was coming to fight him. I told him about Beau's fights with those two knockheads at the river, and the knights with all the different colors. He seems convinced that Beau must be Gawain or Lancelot, too. He yelled at me a bit, told me what he'd do to Beau, you remember, then told three of his soldiers to take me out and hang me in the woods."

"How did you escape? Did Terence help you?"

Roger shook his head. "Nay, but the story's almost as odd. We passed a woodcutter in the forest, a hairy fellow in rough clothes. He heard the soldiers talking about what they meant to do and told them to let me go. They laughed at him, and one of them tried to poke the fellow with his spear. Well, you never saw anything like what happened next. This scruffy peasant just took the spear away from the soldier, bashed all three of them about for a bit, then sent them running back to camp as if they had bears after them. Then the chap broke the spear, tossed it aside, and sent me on my way. He wasn't even breathing hard." Roger paused, staring at the fire. "Anyway, after that it was easy. I found the shed where my horse was and came back here."

"Where do you suppose this woodcutter came from?" asked Lynet.

"I didn't ask, being too busy saying thank you," Roger replied.

The next morning, true to his vow, Beaumains suited up and prepared to go. Sir Persant made a speech that no one listened to, and the half-witted Violet sobbed and wailed. Lynet was still worried that Beaumains was not completely healed, but she was not sorry to leave their host and his daughter. Just before they mounted up and rode off, Lynet stepped forward and said, "Sir Persant, we thank you for your hospitality. You have been very good to us. But now, if I may presume on your good nature, I have one last request."

"Whatever you like!" Sir Persant bellowed.

"Before Beaumains engages this mighty opponent, it seems to me that he deserves to be knighted. Would you bestow this honor on him?"

"With all my heart!" Sir Persant declared. He drew his sword, ready to lay it on Beaumains's shoulders, but Beaumains held up his hand.

For a moment, no one moved, then Roger said, "You'd better go ahead and tell them, Beau."

"Very well," Beaumains said. "Then let it be known that I have been a knight for more than a year. I was made so by none other than the greatest of all knights, Sir Lancelot du Lac."

VIII

The Knight of the Red Lands

"So, I was right!" Lynet murmured to Roger as they rode toward the Castle Perle. "He really is a knight! He's been in disguise all this time!"

"Ay, my lady," Roger said.

Lynet turned toward the dwarf with narrowed eyes. "And you've known it all along?"

Roger nodded.

"How did you know?"

"I'm very clever."

"Roger, I'm serious. How could you know without ever saying a word?"

"I'm clever *and* discreet."

"But when I suggested it, you said it sounded loony," Lynet pointed out.

"And so it is!" Roger said, with feeling. "Just

because it happens to be true doesn't make it less crack-brained!"

"He's not crack-brained," Lynet said automatically, her mind already leaping ahead. "If you knew he was a knight, do you also know his real name?"

Roger was silent, and for a moment Lynet thought he wouldn't answer, but at last he said, "Ay, my lady."

"What is it?" Lynet asked eagerly, glancing once over her shoulder at the lagging Beaumains.

Roger shook his head. "If a man doesn't want his name known, I can respect that. I'm not on the gab. Nor, for that matter, is Kai."

Distracted by the shift in subject, Lynet asked, "Sir Kai?"

"I think Kai's recognized him, too. Doesn't miss much, our Kai. Think about it. From what I hear, Kai was the one who gave him the name Beaumains, which kept everyone from asking his real name. Kai was the one who convinced the king to let him stay, and when Beau volunteered to go with you, Kai was the one who convinced Arthur to let him go and who brought him armor."

It made a sort of sense, but Lynet shook her head. "If Sir Kai knew that he was a knight, why did he mock him so? That wasn't very nice."

"That's just Kai's notion of humor. And remember, Kai was paid back for his mockery."

Lynet said. "True. Beaumains *did* unhorse Sir Kai, didn't he? And Sir Kai is a great knight."

"Ay, my lady."

Lynet thought for a moment. "You've seen both of them, Roger. What are Beaumains's chances with the Knight of the Red Lands?"

"If Beau were whole, I'd say they were good. With that wound in his shoulder, it's a bit trickier, isn't it?" Lynet bit her lip apprehensively, and Roger said gently, "Nay, lass, don't take it so. He'll have his work cut out for him, but he's better than anyone suspects."

Lynet spoke little for the next few hours, thinking about the ordeal that awaited Beaumains and wondering how she would feel if he were to be killed. It was one thing to want an unspecified knight to challenge their enemy, but it was quite another when that knight had a face—a very handsome face—and had been her companion in one way or another for weeks. She wondered, with a start, if she were in love. She decided not to think about the question, but for the first time she was able to sympathize with those who were.

They neared the castle. Lynet began to recognize places where she used to ride in the days before the Red Knight's siege. Suddenly Roger edged his horse in front of hers and stopped. "Don't look, my lady!" he said sharply.

Of course Lynet looked. About thirty yards ahead

of them, hanging limply from a tree, was a man. A few ravens sat on his head and shoulders. She looked away quickly. "Roger?"

"It's what Red Lands does with the knights he kills," Roger said quietly. "They're hanging all around the forest."

Lynet took several deep breaths and felt calmer. "But I didn't see any bodies hanging when I left," she said.

"You left at night, didn't you?"

Lynet nodded and shuddered, realizing that she may have passed beneath any number of those hanging corpses in the dark. Beaumains caught up to them and stared at the body. Roger explained the Red Knight's practice to him, and Beaumains spoke the obvious. "Truly," he said. "He may well be a good knight, but he useth shameful customs."

They rode on, past that dead knight and a half-dozen others, before at last they came out of the forest. Lynet looked across the fields to the Red Knight's siege camp and, beyond the camp, her home, the Castle Perle.

"The Castle Perilous!" Beaumains said, excitement in his voice.

"Yes, well, something like that," Lynet muttered. She had forgotten that she had changed the name back at Camelot as a part of her misguided secrecy.

"Are you ready, lad?" asked Roger suddenly. "We've been seen."

In the siege camp, soldiers and servants were pointing at the newcomers. Beaumains carefully checked
his armor, loosened his sword in its scabbard, and
raised in challenge a lance he had brought from Sir
Persant's camp. More of the Red Knight's servants
scurried about, and Lynet saw them readying a horse.
Last of all, she saw the Knight of the Red Lands himself, donning his armor outside the largest of the tents.

The three travelers rode together up to the Red
Knight's tent, almost in the shadow of the great tower
of the castle. Lynet couldn't help glancing up the wall.
There was Lyonesse, watching from a window.

"For what purpose come ye to this land?" Red
Lands growled.

"Be thou the Knight of the Red Lands?" Beaumains
asked punctiliously.

"I am."

"Then I take leave to call thee a most foul recreant
knight, to so persecute a fair lady and so shamefully
to treat those knights thou defeatest."

"Think well on those hanging knights," the Red
Knight said with a sneer. "Soon you too will adorn
the trees of the forest."

"Don't you mean just one tree?" asked Roger. "I
mean, he's only one knight, after all. You're very im-
precise about these matters, you know."

The Red Knight noticed Roger for the first time.
"You!" he exclaimed.

Roger grinned. "In the flesh. I've brought my knight to you, after all, Red Britches. You remember? The one who just might be Sir Lancelot?"

The Red Knight looked back at Beaumains, a new wariness in his face. "You are the one who defeated the four brethren? And Sir Garard and Sir Arnold of the River?"

"The two chaps at the ford," Roger explained.

"I am," declared Beaumains.

"Then know that I fear thee not! Though thou be Sir Lancelot himself, I shall trample thee under my feet!"

A faint moaning noise emanated from the castle. Lynet recognized it at once as one of her sister's affectations of womanly distress. Sure enough, Lyonesse was leaning out of the castle window, carefully showing her lovely profile to anyone who cared to notice. They all turned to look, and Beaumains made a strangled sound in his throat. His eyes widened, and his jaw dropped.

"Look away from her!" the Red Knight snapped. "She is my lady!"

"Never have I seen such loveliness," Beaumains whispered, still gazing at Lyonesse.

"She's mine, I say!"

"Nay," Beaumains replied breathlessly. His face wore a fierce determination. "She will be mine! For this perfect woman alone will I love all the days of my life. For her I have done many strong battles, and for her sake will I defeat thee!"

Lynet grew cold and still inside. She forced herself to keep her face empty, but when she looked up at her beautiful sister, so frail in appearance but once again victorious, Lynet burned with a hatred that shocked her. At that moment she gladly would have murdered Lyonesse.

A quiet voice beside her said, "I'm sorry, lass."

There was nothing to say. She wanted to act bright and cheerful, but Roger knew better. She raised her chin and smiled.

"That's the dandy, Lynet. As I've said before, I believe you could brazen your way through anything." He leaned forward in his saddle and took her mare's reins. "Come this way, lass. They're about to fight." He led her to one side, while Beaumains and the Red Knight took their places.

Lynet did not remember much of the fight, though she saw every move that Lyonesse made in the window. She was vaguely aware that the knights unhorsed each other with lances, then fought with swords, but beyond that she saw little that happened on the field. From the tower window, Lyonesse watched the battle eagerly, licking her lips occasionally, like a cat. For several minutes Lynet truly hated her sister, but hatred was not natural for Lynet, and at last it ebbed, leaving behind only the ache of despair.

"Hit him, stupid!" muttered Roger, watching the battle beside her. "Don't just stand there, nodcock! If you're going to fight, fight!" He swore bitterly under his breath.

"What is it, Roger?" Lynet asked, forcing her eyes away from her sister.

"He's favoring his left side. I'm afraid the wound may have broken open again." He grunted and added, "Not that I care whether the son of a—whether our dim boy gets bashed about a bit, but we need him to win, or the Red Knight will kill us too."

Lynet had not thought of that. She watched the battle more closely. Roger was right: Beaumains was losing ground. His shield, which was hacked almost in pieces anyway, hung limply at his left side. Only by truly brilliant swordplay, parrying each blow perfectly, was Beaumains surviving the Red Knight's attacks. Suddenly, Beaumains lunged forward, twisting his body to avoid a blow and thrusting with his own sword at the same time. The Red Knight swung his sword and missed, then seemed to freeze. Beaumains's sword had gone into a gap in the Red Knight's armor and was buried deep in the Red Knight's side. Beaumains withdrew his sword, and with a final mighty blow neatly sliced his enemy's head from his shoulders.

Roger urged his horse forward, and Lynet followed. As they drew near, Lynet could hear her sister's voice.

"It was well fought, O knight," she said.

"If I fought well, my lady, it was because I fought for thee, the most beautiful lady in the world," Beaumains gasped. "I offer myself to thee, forever, and I beg thee to open thy gate and receive my heart within!"

Roger made a rude noise. "Disgusting!" he said.

"Ah, now that is a different matter," said Lyonesse. "For before my beloved father's death, I promised him that I would marry no lowborn knight, be he ever so great a fighter."

"That's a lie, Lyon!" Lynet said with a gasp. "You never —"

"It was between Papa and me, sister!" Lyonesse said, squinting fiercely at Lynet. She turned back to Beaumains. "What is thy name, O knight?"

"That I cannot say," Beaumains said, dejected. "Sir Kai called me upon scorn Beaumains, but more than that I cannot reveal. I too have taken a vow."

Lyonesse shrugged. "Then I cannot let you in. Thank you for your help, but I must not allow unknown feet to enter these gates."

Outraged, Lynet cried, "Poppycock, Lyon! This knight has just risked his life for you!"

"I said thank you, didn't I?" Lyonesse replied pettishly. "If he loves me, why won't he tell me his name, then? That's all I ask."

"What do you expect him to do now, then?" demanded Lynet.

"Ride away, I suppose," Lyonesse answered.

"I go then, because thou sayest so," Beaumains answered, despair in his voice. "But know, my lady, that I have never loved any woman before, nor shall I ever love another woman but thee."

Lynet felt Beaumains's words like tiny darts in her heart, and Lyonesse simpered coquettishly from her window. Roger urged his horse forward and nudged Beaumains, none too gently, with his mount's shoulder. "Come on, you blithering ass, let's go. She doesn't want you."

Beaumains turned and staggered dejectedly toward his horse. Roger started to follow, but Lynet said, "Roger?"

He stopped. "Ay, lass?"

"Where will you go?"

Roger shrugged, his face bleak. "We'll find somewhere. Goodbye, my lady." And then Roger rode away with the slumping Beaumains, and Lynet watched them go, wanting to follow but unable to move, wanting to cry but not knowing how, wanting to tell Roger something important but not knowing what.

IX

İn the Other World

As her companions disappeared, Lynet tried frantically to think of a reason to go with them, but she couldn't, so she turned her mare and rode slowly into the Castle Perle. In the stables, she rubbed down her mare, as Roger had taught her, and when she could think of no other task, she reluctantly went into the castle keep.

Lyonesse pounced on her as soon as she entered. "Well? Who is he?" she demanded.

"What are you talking about?" Lynet asked. At the sight of her sister, Lynet's anger had flamed again, but she forced herself to speak calmly.

"My knight, of course!" Lyonesse exclaimed. "You brought him, didn't you? What is his name?"

"He told you. He's called Beaumains."

"Yes, I know that, but what is his real name? Uncle Gringamore says he's too good to be an unknown. He thinks he might even be Gawain or Lancelot in disguise. Is he?"

"I never asked him," Lynet said. "If a man doesn't want to tell his real name, I can respect that." Lyonesse stared at her sister incredulously, but Lynet continued, choosing her words carefully. "What do you care, anyway? You sent him away."

Lyonesse burst into shrill laughter. "Oh, you poor simple girl! Of course I sent him away! If I hadn't, he would have lost interest in me. Men don't want women who are easily won."

"Easily? He almost died for you!"

Lyonesse dismissed this with a toss of her head. "You'll see. He'll be back, begging. In the meantime, I *must* find out who he is! Did he ever say anything that might give us a clue?"

Lynet did not answer. She pushed roughly past her sister and strode down the hall to her own bedchamber. She closed the door firmly and looked dully at the familiar furniture, wondering why it all seemed so strange.

She couldn't stay in her room forever, though, especially once her stomach began to rumble, and so at dinnertime she joined Lyonesse and Sir Gringamore in the small dining room where the family took its meals. Lyonesse acknowledged Lynet's arrival with only the barest of nods, but Sir Gringamore greeted

136

her jovially. "Good to see you, Lynnie. It's been deuced slow here without you," he said.

Lynet chose a seat beside a roast capon and began to help herself. Lyonesse spoke to Sir Gringamore. "All right. We know from the stories that sometimes Sir Lancelot rides in disguise."

"True, true," replied Sir Gringamore. "If you count the time that he wore Sir Kai's armor on a quest. Tristram's gone incognito too, I hear."

"I don't want Sir Tristram," Lyonesse said impatiently. "He's in love with Queen Isoult. I'm sure she's not as pretty as I am, but you know that she and Tristram drank a love potion. He's no good to me." Lynet grimaced at Lyonesse's selfishness, but Lyonesse ignored her. "But this knight might indeed be Sir Lancelot, don't you think?"

"Forget it, Lyon," Lynet said scornfully. "I don't know who he is, but I know he's not Lancelot. He says that Sir Lancelot was the one who knighted him. Besides, I hear that Lancelot's tired of fighting."

Lyonesse pinched her face together in a scowl. Lynet suddenly remembered Lady Eileen's comment about "skinny and peevish-looking" and felt slightly cheered. Lyonesse saw Lynet's smile and misunderstood. "You *do* know something! Tell us, Lynnie! I must know! I can't marry a nobody!"

"Marry?" Lynet said, stunned. "Have you thought

that maybe he doesn't want to marry you, now? Maybe he's realized that you're nothing but a hateful, selfish shrew!"

Sir Gringamore chuckled. "There, see? That's the sort of cozy family chat I've been missing." He looked at Lynet. "If you don't know his name, then do you know someone else who does?"

"Nobody who would tell Lyon," Lynet said deliberately.

Lyonesse scowled again. Suddenly, her brow cleared. "Say, what about that dwarf? The one who brought us the message and who rode away with the knight? Does he know?" Lynet hesitated, and Lyonesse crowed with triumph. "He does, doesn't he! I can see it in your face!"

"It doesn't matter if he does," Lynet retorted. "He won't tell you. He says you're ugly."

Lyonesse's eyes flashed, but she said, "What does a dwarf know about human beauty?"

Lynet rose slowly from her chair. "Roger knows more about beauty than you know about being human," she said in an icy voice. Lyonesse stared wide-eyed at Lynet's hand and swallowed hard. Lynet realized that she was still holding the carving knife and had been pointing it at Lyonesse's breast. She laid the knife down slowly and gathered a few plates of food. "I'll take the rest of my dinner in my room, I think," she said. Neither Lyonesse nor Sir Gringamore spoke as Lynet left the room.

Lynet took most of her meals in her own room for the next few days, avoiding Lyonesse's company. Having gotten away for several weeks, she found castle life unutterably dull and her sister unendurable. Until she had seen Lyonesse callously reject Beaumains's love, she had not realized exactly how cruel her sister could be. If Lyonesse didn't love Beaumains, why did she have to show her profile and capture his heart so effortlessly? She might have left him for someone else, after all. No, it was best that Lynet stay away from Lyonesse, especially when there were carving knives at hand.

In truth, it was not difficult to avoid Lyonesse. After that first night, Lyonesse spent most of her time closeted with Sir Gringamore, talking in whispers and obviously hatching plots. Lynet didn't want to know their schemes, but on the third afternoon, she found that she couldn't avoid Lyonesse's plans entirely. Lynet had decided to take a ride, to get away from the castle at least temporarily, but the head groom stiffly informed her that Lynet was not to be allowed a horse until Lady Lyonesse gave further orders. Furious, and determined not to be Lyonesse's prisoner, Lynet decided that if she couldn't ride, she'd walk.

Brushing by the protesting and clearly discomfited guards at the gate, Lynet strode out into the meadow that until recently had been the camp of the Red Knight. Cold campfires and the usual camp trash lay about, but everything of value had been carted away by the Red Knight's suddenly masterless servants. Beyond the dead camp, just a half mile away, Lynet saw the forest, and she quickened her step. She longed for the purifying scent of pines and the soothing hush of the forest breeze.

When she stepped into the shadows, she immediately felt herself relax, and she was able to breathe deeply again. For hours she wandered among the trees, reflecting nostalgically on her long rides with Roger and Beaumains, and her conversations with the dwarf at their campfires. When the sun began to pale and lower, she regretfully decided that she should be turning toward home. She checked the forest signs that Roger had taught her, determined which direction to go, and had just started to walk when the sound of an axe made her stop. Someone was cutting wood nearby.

Remembering that Roger had been rescued by a woodcutter, Lynet turned toward the sound. She was just about to call out a greeting when she heard a stirring in the bushes behind her. She turned and found herself face to face with three large wolves, sitting on their haunches, watching her.

Slowly she stepped backwards, glancing quickly

around her for some possible weapon, even though she knew in her heart that a lone girl had no chance against three wolves, even a lone girl with a stick. "Shoo!" she said sternly. "Go away!"

The wolves rose to their feet and began to spread out around her. Panicking, she turned and ran wildly through the forest. She heard no following footsteps, but a low growl just behind her indicated the wolves' presence. She knew it was insane to run, but she couldn't stop herself. She burst out of the trees just as one of the wolves pounced. Its forepaws knocked her sprawling into the dirt and pine needles, and she heard a sharp snap as its teeth just missed her ear. Then there was a shout, and the wolves backed away.

Lynet scrambled to a sitting position and looked around. She was in a clearing beside a tiny hut. All around were neat stacks of cut wood. A man with the wildest brown beard that she had ever seen was racing toward her, holding an axe. She shrank away from him, but he ran past her, whispering "Be still," as he went by. He threw himself at the wolves and began laying about him with the axe. The axe flickered like lightning, quicker even than Beaumains's sword, and a wolf lay dead at his feet. Another wolf leaped at him, and the axe flashed again, sinking deep into the wolf's breast. The woodcutter wheeled sharply to face the third wolf, but it lay dead in the dust, an arrow in its heart.

Dazed and disoriented, Lynet looked around the tiny clearing. Behind her and to her right she saw a slender figure lower a longbow. It was Squire Terence. He walked toward her. "Are you hurt, Lady Lynet?" She shook her head, and Terence turned toward the woodsman.

"You are very prompt, sir," the squire said.

"It is nothing," the woodcutter said abruptly. His voice was cultured and even had a trace of a foreign accent. He wiped his axe clean on a dead wolf's fur.

"Thank you, friend," Lynet said to the woodcutter, still dazed. "You saved my life."

"It is nothing," he repeated. He did not look at either of them. When Terence retrieved his arrow from the wolf's carcass, the bearded man turned his face away. "It is not good for a lady to be alone in the forest," he said. "You must go home now."

"I will," Lynet said softly, gathering her wits. "But how can I repay you? I am twice in your debt. You not only saved my life now, but I believe you also saved the life of my friend, Roger the dwarf."

The woodcutter acknowledged the incident with a curt nod, but again he said only, "It is nothing."

"No, it is much. You must let me give you my gratitude. May I know your name?"

The man looked at the ground and said, "I am Jean le Forestier."

Squire Terence smiled suddenly, then bowed deeply.

"I am honored to meet you, Jean le Forestier. I wish you happiness in your new life here." The man looked sharply, searchingly, at Terence, and the squire added, "I will leave you in peace here and say nothing to anyone."

"*Merci,*" whispered Jean.

Terence turned back to Lynet. "Come, my lady. I will take you home now."

Lynet took Terence's outstretched hand and stood. "I must thank you as well, Squire Terence, for you killed one of the wolves."

Terence grinned. "Yes, but I didn't need to." He glanced over his shoulder at Jean le Forestier, who was going into the tiny hut. "If I'd recognized M'sieu Jean before, I'd have let him handle it himself."

"You know him?"

"Yes, my lady. Come this way."

Terence led Lynet into the woods, following a path that only he seemed to see. Lynet stifled the impulse to ask who the woodcutter really was, but she did say, "I take it that he is more than just a woodcutter."

"No one is just a woodcutter," replied Terence. "A person's always more than his present occupation."

"Like you, for instance," Lynet said drily. "You are more than a squire."

"Oh, yes," Terence replied pleasantly.

"I knew the first time I saw you, back at Camelot, that you were more than you seemed." Terence did not answer, and Lynet pressed on. "Roger calls you uncanny and says that you're from the Other World."

"Your friend Roger knows about the Other World, does he? Very interesting fellow, this Roger." Terence flashed Lynet a grin. "You might say that he's more than he seems, as well."

Terence was right. Lynet would have to think more about that when she had time, but now she had other questions. "How did you just happen to be nearby when the wolves attacked, anyway?"

"Nothing very amazing. I've been following you all afternoon. As M'sieu Jean said, it really isn't safe for a lady alone in the forest. And remember, Lady Eileen asked me to keep an eye on you."

"But I never heard a sound!" Lynet exclaimed. Terence only shrugged, and Lynet shook her head. "Roger's right. You *are* uncanny."

They walked on in silence for several minutes as the forest darkened around them. A soft, continuous sound came to Lynet's attention, and it grew louder as they walked. A moment later they stepped out of the woods onto the bank of a small river. A smooth curtain of water flowed over a long flat rock, forming a waterfall about five feet high.

"Where are we?" Lynet asked. "I've never seen this before."

"I know. Come, Lady Lynet. We have to go through the water."

"I thought you said you were taking me back to the Castle," Lynet protested.

"Oh no," Terence said amiably. "I said I would take you home. This way." He pointed straight at the waterfall and held out his hand. Lynet hesitated only a second, then took his hand and walked with him into the cool water. They waded into the shallow river, then walked right through the curtain of falling water, where the mouth of a cave lay concealed behind the translucent falls. Lynet's heart pounded, but with excitement, not fear. Stooping, Terence led her into the opening, then stood in a wide, dry cavern. A torch on the wall lit the room. Lynet brushed her wet hair out of her face and looked around. On the walls were curious inscriptions and carved likenesses of animals. "Just down this passageway," Terence said. "Morgan's waiting."

"Morgan?"

"Morgan Le Fay, Gawain's aunt. I've asked her to show you some of her arts."

"What arts?" Lynet asked, confused.

"She's a sorceress." Lynet gasped, and Terence quickly added, "Don't worry. Not all sorceresses are bad. There are many who do great good. I hope that you will be that sort."

"Me? A sorceress?"

Terence nodded. "Whether you like it or not," he said gently. "Here we are."

They stepped around a black rock into a large cavern. There, in the orange glow of several torches and one large fire, stood the most beautiful woman Lynet had ever seen. The woman scowled. "At last! I've been waiting this two hours and more!" Terence smiled, but didn't answer. The woman looked at Lynet. "This is the one?"

"As you see, my lady," replied Terence.

"Hmm. Yes, I can see it now that I look at her. But I'll wager she doesn't know much."

"Why then, I'm glad that I chose for her a patient teacher," replied Terence. It seemed odd to Lynet, but the soft-spoken squire at her side seemed to be rebuking this majestic woman.

The lady pursed her lips, then curtsied elaborately. "I understand you, your grace. We're in your dominion now, so I'll be good. But allow me to say that I like you better back in the World of Men, serving drinks in Gawain's chambers."

Terence laughed quietly. "I don't doubt it," he said.

"*Back* in the World of Men?" asked Lynet faintly.

"You're in the Other World now, my lady," Terence replied. "I'll leave you now. Don't let Lady Morgan frighten you. She's not as fierce as she pretends to be." And then Terence slipped away down a passageway.

Lynet could not have told how long she spent in that cavern with Morgan Le Fay. Without the sun and moon to mark the days, time seemed unimportant. At first, Lynet had been hesitant before Morgan's awe-inspiring presence, but it was not in Lynet's nature to be timorous for long. Besides, Lynet soon learned that Terence was right: beneath Morgan's grand façade, she was capable of warm feelings and even generosity toward those she liked, and it soon became clear to Lynet that *she* was one of that select few.

Much of their time together, Morgan simply told stories. She told of faeries and spells, of strange creatures, of men and women who traveled easily between worlds and who were consequently considered wizards and magicians. "Remember that, Lynet," Morgan said. "What is called magic in the World of Men is called that only because it does not belong there. Powers and actions that are miraculous in that place are perfectly normal here."

"You mean in this world it's normal to turn people into toads or whatever it is sorceresses do?"

"The toad trick is a bit childish, but no, it would not be considered odd here." Morgan smiled suddenly. "Do you want to change someone into a toad?"

Lynet thought briefly, with a flash of pleasure, about how her sister would look as a toad, but she shook her head. "I suppose not," she said.

"If you don't care for toads, we have other spells. Rats? Pigeons? Dragons? Dwarfs? You'll be learning all these spells soon."

147

"You can change a person into a dwarf?" Lynet asked, surprised.

"I've never done it myself, but it's in the books. All this will come in time."

Lynet shook her head wonderingly and said nothing.

Gradually Lynet came to realize that Morgan's stories all had their reasons, though she was not able to put every story's lesson into words. She said as much to Morgan, and the enchantress nodded briefly. "In this world, almost everything is taught with stories. Much more to the point than the sort of silliness that passes for education in that other place, don't you think?"

Many of Morgan's stories were about sorceresses, beginning with the first enchantress of all, the faery queen Lilith. Lynet listened with awe to tales of cruel, grasping witches and to others about kindly magical princesses. Once she exclaimed, "But I always thought that sorceresses were evil!"

"What do you mean, 'evil'?"

Lynet had never considered the question. "You know," she said, after a moment, "unfriendly to people."

"People!" repeated Morgan derisively. "As if humans were all that mattered. Just once I'd like to see people judged by how friendly they are to sorceresses."

Lynet could not help smiling, but she said, "But we do judge people by how they treat animals and servants and those that are weaker than they. So why not judge sorceresses by how they treat people?"

Morgan frowned and looked sourly at Lynet. At last she said, "Let's not forget which of us is the teacher, dear. Back to your question — no, not all sorceresses are, as you say, unfriendly to people. But the strongest ones are."

"Why is that?"

"The enchantress who cares for no one cannot be touched by grief or worry or fear. Nothing reduces a sorceress's power so much as love."

"Do you love anyone?" Lynet asked.

Morgan's brow furrowed very slightly, then smoothed. "We are not discussing me. Do you?"

Lynet thought of Beaumains's handsome profile and felt her own brow furrow. She and Morgan were silent together for a long time.

Sometimes they would grow weary of tales. Then they would gradually grow quiet, then lapse together into a comfortable slumber on the soft dirt floor of the cavern. When they awoke, they would resume their conversation wherever they had left off, as if they had never slept.

At last, Morgan said, "I think I've done. You will never stop learning, but I've taught you what you must know, and I've never had so apt a pupil. You will never be an enchantress like me, of course." Lynet raised her eyebrows, a bit indignant, but Morgan added, "I don't mean that you'll be lesser, only different. You like humans too much."

"Well, I *am* one, you see," Lynet said apologetically.

"Are you?"

"Well, of course I . . . what do you mean?"

"Your father was Duke Idres, was he not?" Lynet nodded, waiting. "He was well known in this world. His mother — your grandmother — was a notable enchantress, from a distinguished faery family."

"I never knew her," Lynet murmured. "Then I am part faery?"

"You are. You may never have known it, but anyone from this world could see it in you at a glance. You have the look."

"That's what Terence said," Lynet replied.

Morgan nodded. "Terence would know. He is from a very great faery family himself. He is, in fact, the Duke of Avalon."

Lynet blinked with astonishment. "And he serves as a squire in the World of Men?" she asked faintly.

"Don't ask me," Morgan said. "I don't understand it either. Anyway, the point is that you are only part human."

Lynet frowned suddenly. "But doesn't that mean that my sister is also part faery?"

"In theory," Morgan admitted, "but not really. Even in families where the faery strain is strong, you never know where it will come out. In my own family, my sisters and I are enchantresses, but among my nephews only Gawain shows his faery blood. As for his brothers Gaheris, Agrivaine, and especially that nincompoop Gareth, they're as earthbound as mud clods. And your sister, well, she's far too foolish to be anything but pure human, as you'll soon be able to observe firsthand. It is time you went back to that other place."

"You mean home?"

Morgan shook her head. "You don't know it yet, but that isn't your home anymore. This is. But for now, to keep you from homesickness, you are permitted to take a gift with you. Let me show you something." Morgan rolled aside a rock, revealing a small hole in the cavern wall. From the hole, she took out three bottles. "These are three elixers, each with its own powers, none to be taken lightly. You may choose one for your own."

"What are they?"

Morgan lifted the first bottle. "This one is a love potion."

Lynet stared at the amber liquid inside. "I thought you said that to love someone made a sorceress weak," she asked.

"Heavens, girl, don't ever take the stuff yourself. But it doesn't hurt a sorceress's powers to be adored by someone else. All you do is put a drop in a man's drink, and the next person that he sees he will love until the end of his life. Have you anyone you'd like to enslave?"

Lynet held her breath. She had only to close her eyes to see Beaumains's eyes, as they gazed adoringly at Lyonesse. When Lynet thought that she could see him gaze at her in that way, she felt almost giddy. She started to reach for the bottle, but Morgan said, "Just a moment. You ought to know the dangers."

Lynet let her hand drop, but she kept her eyes on the bottle. "What dangers?"

"First, you must make sure that the subject sees the right person immediately after taking the potion. If he sees someone else, you've made a terrible mess. That's what happened with Sir Tristram and Queen Isoult: the potion was meant for Isoult's husband, but Tristram mucked it up. And that's not even the worst danger. You see, there's no cure."

"Why is that a problem?" Lynet asked.

"Just this," Morgan said. "If you use the potion, make sure that you use it on someone you won't mind having around for the rest of your life."

Strangely enough, Lynet realized, she had never thought about the rest of her life. When she dreamed of the tall young Beaumains, she imagined the moment when he would declare his love for her, but she had never really considered what came after that. For a moment, she envisioned herself and Beaumains, middle-aged, sitting by a fire on a winter evening. What would they talk about? Her cherished picture of Beaumains seemed suddenly blurred. "I'll have to think about that," she admitted to Morgan. "What are the other potions?"

Morgan lifted the second vial, filled with a ruby red elixir. "This potion will give you beauty beyond that of any mere mortal woman. Much more practical than the love potion, I might add. With such beauty you can make anyone you like fall in love with you anyway, but there's no tiresome spell forcing the issue. What do you think?" Lynet hesitated, and Morgan seemed to read her thoughts. "Be a bit of a shock for your sister, wouldn't it?"

She was right. It would almost kill poor Lyonesse if Lynet showed up more beautiful than she was. And of course, if Beaumains had fallen in love with Lyonesse's beauty, why should he not do the same for a suddenly ravishing Lynet? Peeking at Morgan, Lynet had a sudden insight into her teacher's stunning beauty. It was tempting, but for some reason Lynet hesitated. "What is the third elixir?"

"This," Morgan said, holding up a crystal bottle filled with a clear liquid, "is a healing potion. Whatever illness, whatever wound a person has, this potion will cure it. But it has bothersome limits."

"What limits?"

"It cannot bring back one who is dead. After

you've used it on a person, you can never use it on that person again—no one cheats death forever. And finally, you cannot use it on yourself." Morgan paused, then added wryly, "As you might imagine, this one's not the most popular choice among new enchantresses."

Lynet said, "I'll take that one."

It was surprisingly difficult to say goodbye to Morgan. Although the sorceress was frequently cool and unapproachable, Lynet discovered that she felt closer to this faery beauty than she had ever felt to her own sister. So it was with a leaden step that she returned to the waterfall at the cave mouth, where the World of Men began. But taking a breath, Lynet stepped resolutely through the rainbow-streaked veil of water, into the glory of a sunny day. At first, all she could do was rub her eyes and blink in the unaccustomed light, but when at last she could see, she smiled, because Terence and Robin were on the riverbank waiting for her.

"Hallo, my dear," Robin chirped. "Lovely day for bathing."

"Hello, Robin," Lynet said, smiling. "And hello, your grace."

"You're looking well, my lady," replied Terence. "I take it that Lady Morgan wasn't too unkind."

"I think she could be," Lynet said thoughtfully. "But she never was to me. What time is it? When I went into the cave, it was almost dark, and now it's full day. Was I there overnight?"

Robin giggled. "Ay, my lady, you could say that."

"Be quiet, Robin," Terence said. He turned to Lynet. "It's a bit difficult to tell how time has passed when you're between worlds, isn't it? You've been gone almost a fortnight."

Lynet gasped. "A fortnight!" she repeated in a whisper.

"It's not so bad, my lady," Terence said reassuringly. "The last time Gawain and I went home for a visit, we found that seven years had gone by when we returned here. We've had to give up birthday parties, because we don't know how old we are. Don't worry, though. Your sister and uncle haven't been worried."

"I doubt they missed me at all," Lynet said. A sudden hope occurred to her. "Do I . . . must I go back to them? Now that I'm away, couldn't I go somewhere else?"

"Oh, I wouldn't do that," Robin said. "Things are just getting interesting back at the castle. That's why my lord duke Terence commanded me to be here. I'm to send you home at once."

"I just asked a favor for a friend," Terence protested mildly.

"But what's going on back at the castle?" Lynet asked.

Robin looked at Terence, who nodded. Robin said,

"Your uncle has just captured someone whom he plans to torture to make him reveal a secret."

"What captive? What secret?"

This time it was Terence who answered. "It's your friend Roger."

X

THE NIGHT OF
THE HALF MOON

Evidently, transporting people across great distances was a part of Robin's particular magic, because one moment Lynet was watching Robin's laughing face, and then the forest seem to darken and grow solid around her, and she found herself enclosed by gray stone in her own bedchamber back at the Castle Perle.

At first all she could do was grip her bedpost, as if it were a support against an unstable world. After a moment, though, the muffled sound of two voices in the corridor recalled her to her position. Even through the heavy oaken door, Lynet easily recognized one voice as Lyonesse's. Crossing the room in a few swift strides, she threw open the door and stepped into the hallway. Lyonesse and Sir Gringamore stopped talking and stared at her.

"What have you done with Roger?" Lynet demanded.

"Goodness, Lynet," replied Lyonesse. "Have you been in your room all this time? Really, it isn't healthy. Why, I haven't seen you in almost a week."

"Two weeks," corrected Sir Gringamore. "Bribed one of the servants to bring your food to your room, did you? Well, well, that's none of my affair, as long as you haven't been into the wine. You haven't, have you?"

"I asked you a question!" Lynet snapped. "Where's Roger?"

"I haven't a notion what you're talking about," Lyonesse said. "None of my young men are named...do you mean that Sir Beaumains is really named Roger?"

"Never heard of any Sir Roger," Sir Gringamore said, considering this. "Could be a new fellow, of course, but it sounds rather plebeian to me."

"Roger's not a knight!" Lynet said.

"Well, what's the use of him then?" replied Lyonesse practically. "Really, Lynet, it's not at all the thing to burst out of your room and interrupt a private conversation. Do go away."

Sir Gringamore laughed pleasantly. "Sisterly love," he murmured.

Realizing that she couldn't penetrate Lyonesse's self-absorption with mere words, Lynet stepped closer, took Lyonesse's dress in her hands, and shook her sister violently. "Where-is-Roger?" she demanded again.

Lyonesse pulled away and staggered back against the

corridor wall. In the light of the lamp in a nearby wall sconce, her eyes flamed with equal parts of fear and anger. "I don't know, I tell you! Who is this Roger?"

"Roger the dwarf," Lynet said.

Lyonesse's eyes flickered toward Sir Gringamore, whose stolid face showed nothing. With a trilling, nervous laugh, Lyonesse said, "What dwarf?"

"The dwarf Uncle Gringamore captured for you."

Lyonesse's eyes widened, and she glanced again at Sir Gringamore. "I don't know what you're talking about," she said weakly. "We don't have anyone in our dungeon at all."

"You put him in the dungeon?" Lynet gasped. Turning on her heel, she strode quickly down the corridor toward the stairs that led to the castle's small dungeon.

Behind her, she heard Sir Gringamore say placidly, "You know, my dear, all those beauty oils you put on your face must have soaked into your brain. How came you to say such a henwitted thing?" Lyonesse snapped something at him in an irritated tone, but Lynet was already out of earshot. She stormed down the dungeon stairs and went at once to the nearest door.

"Roger?" she whispered.

"Hallo, lass," came the cheerful reply. "Did you send for me?"

Lynet unbarred the door and went in. "Don't be a fool. You can't think I had anything to do with this.

My sister is an idiot." The room was dark, and she couldn't see where Roger was.

"Ah, but you did have something to do with it," said Roger, his voice coming from the far wall. "Your uncle — quite a pleasant chap, even if he did drag me here in a burlap bag — said that you told them I knew Beaumains's real name."

Lynet was silent for a moment. "He's right, I did, just to annoy them. But I never thought they'd kidnap you. Here, you can come out now."

"Well, it's nice of you to say so, but there are these chains to deal with."

"You don't mean to say they chained you up, too! I'll kill her!"

"Suits me," Roger replied. "But before you go, could you bring me a stool? These arm shackles are a bit high for a dwarf, and it's rather uncomfortable, just hanging like this."

Lynet's eyes had grown accustomed to the gloom, and she could make out a dark shape suspended half-way up the wall. With a cry of indignation, she whirled on her heel to find a stool, after which she intended to choke Lyonesse until she could get the key to the shackles. Both of these noble intentions were foiled, however, because as she turned she ran right into the soft but formidable form of Sir Gringamore, who had followed her, bringing a bright torch.

"Tut, tut, Lynnie. Always so hasty. Let's just talk about all this for a moment."

"I don't want to talk!"

"Well, you ought to anyway," he replied, imperturbably. "You want your friend released, don't you?"

This halted her. "Yes."

"Well, maybe you can convince him to tell us what we need to know."

"I'll do no such thing. Let me by. I need to get something for him to stand on. His arms must feel as if they're breaking."

She started to push by, but Sir Gringamore grabbed her upper arm and held her. "No, Lynnie. That's what we want. The more uncomfortable he is, the sooner he'll talk."

Lynet turned her fulminating gaze at Sir Gringamore and said very slowly, "Take your hand off of me, uncle, or I'll turn you into the toad that you really are."

Lyonesse, entering the room behind Sir Gringamore, tittered at Lynet's threat, but Sir Gringamore snatched his hand away and peered closely at Lynet. "You're serious, aren't you? Deuce it, I always thought you had too much of your father in you. You've been up to something wicked and magical, I'll be bound."

"Step aside," Lynet said, and Sir Gringamore obeyed.

Lynet returned a moment later with a chair for

Roger to stand on. He sighed with relief and said, "Thankee, lass."

"Now," said Lynet, turning to face her uncle and sister, "give me the keys."

"Not until he tells us the knight's name!" Lyonesse said angrily.

Lynet started toward her sister, hands already raised at throat level, but Sir Gringamore stepped between the sisters. "Now, now, my dear," Sir Gringamore said, chuckling slightly. "I don't think that's necessary. We only wanted to scare this dwarf, but it failed. We may as well let him go now."

"I thought we were going to torture—" Lyonesse began.

"You most certainly will *not!*" declared Lynet.

"Quite right, quite right," intervened Sir Gringamore. "No question of torture at all. Lynnie, will you go get the keys to the shackles?"

Lynet had turned toward her sister again, but at these words she stopped. "Yes, of course. Where are they?" she asked, relieved.

"Hmm? Oh, they're right next door. In the next dungeon room, on the cot."

Quickly, Lynet walked into the other room. Away from Sir Gringamore's torch, she could see nothing, but she felt her way across the room, looking for the cot Sir Gringamore had mentioned. "Could you bring the torch in here, uncle?" she called from the blackness.

"Just coming," he answered. Lynet saw the glow of the torch as it rounded the corner. Then the door to the dungeon room closed, and she heard the bolt fall into place.

Incredulous, Lynet said, "Uncle?"

"Sorry, Lynnie, but it seemed the best thing to do. You'll be safe enough in there until we've gotten this dwarf to talk."

For the next few minutes, Lynet called her uncle and sister every name she could think of, using vocabulary that she had not even been aware that she knew, but at last she ran out of inventiveness and lapsed into panting silence.

Sir Gringamore chuckled. "That's what comes of letting a girl hang about the stables. Splendidly done, Lynnie. Really very imaginative. But if you've finished, we need to talk to this fellow. Now, master dwarf, won't you just save us all some trouble and tell us who this chap Beaumains really is?"

"I'd be happy to," Roger said calmly.

"What?" gasped Lyonesse, taken by surprise. "You will?"

"Of course. Keeping a secret is all well and good, but the Beau's not worth it. Let Lynet go; I'll gladly trade a fool's secret for a lady's freedom."

Roger paused, then said clearly, "The knight we call Beaumains is really Sir Gareth of Orkney. He is a royal prince of Orkney, the youngest brother of the great Sir Gawain, and one of the finest fighters in Arthur's court."

Lynet knew at once that Roger was telling the truth. Everything fit. She remembered what Terence had told her, how Gareth had made some vow and left the court. So that was why Beaumains had let his hair and beard grow over his face when he returned to court: he didn't want to be known until he had fulfilled his vow. And that was why he had avoided Terence when they met him in the forest: Who would be more likely to recognize him, now that he was clean-shaven, than his brother Gawain's squire? Lynet felt slightly dizzy as she realized the smelly kitchen knave she had ridden with, who had rescued her from the Black Knight, was actually a prince, from one of the oldest and most respected families in all England.

Lynet was not the only person to make this connection, of course. Lyonesse was fairly cackling with excitement. "A royal prince!" she crowed. "Brother of Sir Gawain! Why, that would make him King Arthur's nephew!"

"That it would," replied Sir Gringamore. "Quite a catch, eh?"

Lyonesse chortled and lapsed into an affected tone of voice. "'Why, hello, Guinevere! Charming to see you today. And how's Uncle Arthur today?' Why, when we're married, I'll be a crown princess!"

"If you can catch him," Sir Gringamore said.

"You'd best make sure of him before he gets away. Dwarf, where is your master now?"

"He's not my master."

At that very moment, as if the whole scene had been orchestrated, a soldier came down the steps to the dungeon rooms. "Sir Gringamore? Is that you?"

"Yes, but as you can see, I'm busy," Sir Gringamore snapped.

"Yes, sir. Of course, sir. But this knight was saying as how he'd burn the castle down, and the captain thought it best to tell—"

"Knight? What knight?"

The soldier sounded relieved that Sir Gringamore was interested. "I don't know him, sir, but he says that you've stolen his dwarf."

Sir Gringamore smiled brightly. "All nonsense, of course."

"Yes, sir. We told him that, sir, but this Sir Beaumains won't leave. Um . . . what should we do?"

With triumph in her voice, Lyonesse said, "Invite him in for dinner, of course."

Dinner was a wretched experience for Lynet. To begin with, she arrived late. As soon as Sir Gringamore released them both, Lynet took Roger up to her bedchamber, where she had a salve to rub on the dwarf's chafed wrists. While she treated his abrasions, Roger told her what had been happening since they parted.

He and Beaumains — Gareth, now — had ridden a half day into the woods, where Gareth had collapsed, weak from his battle with the Knight of the Red Lands. Roger had found a deserted cottage, where they had lived for two weeks, eating dried meat they found in the larder and whatever Roger could rustle up from the forest, while Gareth recuperated.

He recovered quickly, and they made ready to travel, but the day before they were to leave, Roger had been captured. He had heard a hunting party in the woods, and he had crept closer to look. He had barely had time to recognize Sir Gringamore at the head of the party when a sack had been dropped over his head. "They all thought it was a great joke," he said, in conclusion. "They'd been expecting to follow our trail for weeks, before they could have a chance to capture me, and here they'd gotten me on their first day out. Luck. I've always been lucky, I guess."

Lynet pretended not to notice the bitterness in Roger's voice and finished wrapping up his wrists. "There. Now we're late for dinner. What do you think will happen? What will Beaumains — Gareth, I mean — do? Will he be very angry about their kidnaping you?"

Roger took a breath. "Well, if you want to know the truth, I think the Beau's probably forgotten about me. For two weeks all he's talked about is your sister." Roger's voice was gentle. "I thought it best to warn you. I imagine that he's already making puppy eyes at that cat."

Lynet nodded. "Of course," she said quietly. "And Lyonesse will be encouraging him in every outrageous way."

And so it was. When they arrived in the dining room, Gareth did not even look up. His eyes were fixed on Lyonesse, and Lyonesse, for her part, was seeing to it that they stayed there. Lynet sat and ate her dinner without a word, while Gareth and Lyonesse uttered fatuous compliments to each other.

For a moment, Lynet wished that back in the cave she had chosen the cordial that would make her beautiful. Maybe *that* would take the wind out of Lyonesse's sails. But at heart she knew that Lyonesse had captured Gareth with more than just beauty. Watching Lyonesse titter and blush and flutter her eyelashes and fawn over Gareth, Lynet knew that she could never match such a performance. And, though she was disappointed with Gareth, that he could be won with such tactics, she couldn't say she was surprised. While Gareth's handsome face was enough to sway any female's affections — well, it had swayed hers, after all — Lynet had to admit that he really wasn't the cleverest fellow around.

In fact, Lynet realized with faint surprise, she had fallen out of love with Gareth as quickly and as easily as she had fallen in love with him in the first place.

While she still felt a certain fondness for him, as a familiar traveling companion, she no longer thought of him romantically. Maybe her change of heart had begun when Gareth declared his love for Lyonesse, or maybe it had arisen in the enchantress's cave, when Lynet had imagined a lifetime with Beaumains. Whatever the reason, she was no longer in love, and the effusive dalliance that Gareth and Lyonesse were carrying on before her was not painful, only embarrassing.

Then, just before the third course, the flirting moved from embarrassing to shocking: Lynet overheard Lyonesse whisper, "Then it's settled. I'll come to your room tonight, at midnight."

Lynet stood in the moonlight at the casement window of her room. The night air was heavy and fragrant, like one of Morgan's potions. Perhaps a sleeping potion: Sir Gringamore was snoring off his wine in the banquet hall, and the last of the servants had stumbled across the courtyard toward their beds over an hour before. But Lynet had never felt more awake. She gazed amiably at the half moon. What was it Robin had said? That the half moon was a night for good magic? Lynet felt a tingle of excitement and smiled. Maybe she was an enchantress at heart after all.

Then the nighttime peace was split apart with loud, terrified female screams. Lynet leaped from her chair, threw open her door, and raced barefoot down the hall toward the source of the sound — Gareth's room. Bursting through the door, she encountered a scene of utter mayhem. Lyonesse, barely clothed, cowered in a far corner of the room, shrieking as if mad. In the center of the room, a bare-chested Gareth stood facing a fully armored and helmeted knight. Gareth was unarmed, but the other knight held a sword at Gareth's throat.

"What's going on?" Lynet demanded.

"Good evening, ma'am," the strange knight replied. "Sorry to disturb you, but I won't be a minute. I'm just here to kill this worthless piece of carrion."

"Which one?" Lynet asked practically.

"Sir Gareth, of course. Do you think you could do something with your sister? I believe she's gone quite mad."

Moving very slowly, Lynet circled the room, staying close to the wall, until she came to Lyonesse. "Lyon, please stop screaming — Lyon, I know it's frightening, but — oh, do shut up, Lyon!"

Lyonesse ceased screaming for a second, then burst into hysterical sobs. "I'm sorry, father! He seduced me! He forced me to come to his room! You know I would never do anything like this unless I were forced!" She sank to her knees, still sobbing.

Lynet realized for the first time that the knight who held the sword at Gareth's throat was wearing her father's armor. "Sir knight," Lynet said slowly, a chill creeping up her back, "she fears you because you are wearing our father's armor."

"Oh yes, well, I'm sorry about that. It was all I could find in a pinch. You don't mind, do you?"

A wave of relief swept over Lynet. This was no ghost. "No, of course not," she answered automatically. Then, realizing how silly the whole exchange was, she giggled. The knight chuckled, and while he was distracted, Gareth leaped across the room and snatched up his own sword.

"Now," Gareth said hoarsely, "let us see who shall kill who!"

"Whom, you stupid sod. Who shall kill *whom*," the knight retorted, swinging his sword heavily at Gareth. Gareth deflected the blow easily and knocked the strange knight backwards with a mighty chop. Then Gareth lunged forward, following up his advantage, and the strange knight barely eluded a blow that would have ended the fight at once. Then the fight settled down, following a pattern that Lynet easily recognized. It was like Gareth's battle with the pink knight and the fish: Gareth attacked, but the other knight was content merely to defend himself. Gareth began to pant, and the other knight laughed softly. "Out of shape, aren't we, Gareth? It doesn't do much for your muscles, all this lying about with loose women, does it?"

With a roar, Gareth leaped forward, shouting, "She's not a loose woman!"

The strange knight sidestepped Gareth's reckless charge and had he been quicker, would have landed a blow on Gareth's unprotected shoulder. "Who, this trollope?" the strange knight taunted. "Of course she's a loose woman! She came to your room at midnight, didn't she? She's a doxy, a jade, a bit of painted muslin."

Again Gareth attacked angrily, but more cautiously this time, and the strange knight had no chance to inflict any damage. "And for Gog's sake, Gareth, you ought to know a wanton woman. After all, your mother was one."

With a shriek of inhuman rage, Gareth cast himself at the mocking knight, swinging his sword wildly. The strange knight took several blows, each one denting his armor, but he was able to land one blow of his own, on Gareth's thigh. It looked superficial, but the pain of it shocked Gareth back to his senses, and he backed away.

"Had enough?" the strange knight gasped. "Wouldn't you rather be back in bed?" Gareth did not answer, circling warily, and the strange knight tried a new tack. "I wouldn't be so eager to crawl into bed with little Gareth, my lady," he called to Lyonesse. "He wets the bed."

"What?" Gareth gasped.

"S'truth, my lady. Always did. None of his brothers would ever double up with him, on account of the cold spots he left."

"Who are you?" Gareth said, barely above a whisper.

The strange knight's voice was cold and even. "I'm your worst nightmare, you foul-smelling, vomitous rat, you son of a witch!"

Gareth launched himself at the knight, screaming insanely. It seemed to Lynet that the strange knight made no effort to defend himself but instead was focused wholly on inflicting a certain wound on Gareth. As Gareth swung his sword at the knight's neck, the knight lunged forward and cut a deep gash in Gareth's inner thigh. But Gareth's blow landed on the strange knight's neck and shoulder. He staggered back against the wall, and in the moonlight Lynet could see blood welling up over the knight's breastplate.

Acting instinctively, Lynet dashed across to the wounded knight, almost hurdling Gareth to get to him. "Thankee, my lady, but I think you're wasting your time," the knight managed to gasp as she arrived. "He's cut my veins through."

At once Lynet remembered her cordial, back in her room, her gift from the enchantress's cave. "I won't let you die!" she said fiercely. "Come with me!" She pulled the knight forward, tugging him after her, praying that he would be able to stay on his feet. She was only vaguely aware of Gareth, sprawled on the floor, clutching his wounded leg, and then she and the knight were in the corridor, staggering together toward Lynet's room.

How they got there, Lynet would never know, but somehow they both stayed on their feet long enough to make it to her door, and then the knight collapsed on the floor. Lynet snatched up the cordial. "Stay alive just another moment," she begged, fumbling at the lid.

"I can't," the knight whispered. "But it was worth it. He won't be feeling...amorous...for a long time now."

"Shut up and take your helm off," Lynet said briskly. She tore at the straps and pulled the helm off. "Oh!" she cried in amazement.

It was no stranger. It was the young man she had seen beside the stream on the night she gathered herbs with Robin, the tall man whose face had betrayed such inexpressible sadness.

Lynet shook her head sharply, banishing her wonder, and poured the cordial over the gaping wound in the knight's neck. Where it touched the knight's skin, it sizzled as if it were liquid fire, and the knight twitched with pain, but then he blinked, raised a gauntleted hand to his neck and said, "Good Gog, lass! What have you done?"

"I've cured you, of course."

"It's like magic," he said.

"It *is* magic, stupid," she retorted. "Now, tell me. Who are you?"

The knight was silent. He sat up and looked around. "You've cured me! You've—" He broke off sharply as he looked out the window. Suddenly full of energy, he scrambled to his feet and leaped to the window, staring at the moon. "It's after two o'clock," he said, amazement in his voice.

"Very likely," Lynet said patiently. "Now, who are you?"

The knight turned back to her, his eyes warm and his lips curling in a soft smile. For some reason, Lynet had difficulty breathing. "You don't understand," the young man said. "At two o'clock, I was supposed to disappear and become someone else."

"Well, don't do it for my sake," Lynet said, forcing herself to breathe evenly. "I still don't know who you are now."

The young man stepped forward and took her hands. "You see, I've been rather under a spell. It's made me appear in a different shape, except for two hours, twice a month—from midnight until two when the moon is at the half-face. But you must have broken the spell. I'm still in my true form."

"Your true form?" Lynet repeated, confused. "So what have you been?"

"I've been a dwarf named Roger," the young man replied simply.

Lynet stepped backwards, pulling her hands away and clutching the bedpost, sinking slowly down onto her bed. "Roger?" she said faintly.

He smiled. "Ay, lass. S'truth."

"You're Roger?" she repeated.

"Not anymore," the young man said, taking her hands again.

"Yes, of course...but...well, what's your real name, then?"

"My name is Gaheris," he replied.

XI

GAHERIS'S STORY

For a long time, Lynet could only stare. Then she closed her bedroom door and said, "Sit down and explain yourself, please, before I go mad."

Gaheris nodded. He turned the chair to face the bed and sat, while Lynet made herself comfortable on the bed. "It was the way that clodpole Gareth treated you. That was what set me off," he began. "The way he ignored you at dinner this evening! And making that appointment with —"

"No, no, I don't care about that. Tell me *your* story. However did you come to be changed into a dwarf?"

"Oh, well, that was the witch. I suppose I should say enchantress. They all want to be called enchantresses. Mother always did, and so does Morgan. Morgan's my aunt. She's —"

"I know your Aunt Morgan very well," Lynet interposed.

"Do you? Bit of a pill, isn't she?"

"I rather like her," Lynet protested. "Was your mother like Morgan?"

"Oh, heavens, no! Mother was..." Gaheris trailed off. "Look here, I'm making a mull of this. I'd better start at the very beginning, hadn't I?"

Lynet nodded. Gaheris settled himself comfortably in the chair, took a deep breath and began.

"I was born into an unfortunate household," he said. Lynet started to comment on this statement, but Gaheris hurried on. "Oh, I know what you're thinking. I was born a prince, wasn't I? But there are other sorts of misfortune.

"I barely remember my father. He died when I was twelve, but even before he died, I hardly ever saw him. He was always off fighting in the wars, trying to win some new plot of land for Mother to rule. Father was a good man, I think, but his will was no match for Mother's.

"Occasionally, when he was home, he'd take my brother Gawain and me out to the fields to teach us knighthood. It was a good thing for a father to do, but even those times were a trial to me. You see, I'm not much good with a sword. Or...or any weapon, I suppose."

"I remember," Lynet murmured.

"Ay, you would. I think that was my lowest moment, when you took my sword away from me and stole my dinner."

"I didn't steal it!" Lynet exclaimed. "I shared it with you, didn't I?"

"Beg pardon, my lady," Gaheris said meekly. "Very kind of you, I'm sure."

"It was burned anyway," Lynet muttered. "Go on."

"Well, as I say, I was an absolute oaf with weapons. And to make things worse, Gawain was naturally gifted. By the time he was sixteen, he was a match for Father, and they could spar together as equals. Me, I could barely hold a sword and walk at the same time. I was, as Gawain told me so often, hopeless."

"What a terrible thing to say!" Lynet said indignantly.

"Nay, don't hold it against Gawain," Gaheris said. "He's my favorite brother. But you see how it must have appeared to him. He did things by instinct that I couldn't do even after hours of teaching. He was in constant despair over me.

"And then there was Mother." Gaheris's face grew bleak, and he was silent for a long time.

"She was an enchantress too, wasn't she?" Lynet said at last, hoping to rouse him from his bitter reverie.

"Ay. The worst kind. She cared nothing for any of

us, but only for her magic and, most of all, for power. We were raised by servants, mostly. Mother cared for no one, but she hated me."

"Why you in particular?"

"I don't know. Maybe because I saw through her. As early as I can remember, I knew that she despised us. My younger brothers, Agrivaine and Gareth, believed that she loved them, and they would fall all over themselves to win her favor, but I wouldn't."

"How could a mother hate her own child?"

"Hating came naturally to Mother," Gaheris replied. "It was what made her strong." Lynet remembered what Morgan had told her in the cave, that love would only weaken an enchantress. She shook her head slowly: It was too much to pay for power. Gaheris continued. "Then Father died, fighting against King Arthur. That was Mother's doing, too, of course. Father liked Arthur, but Mother couldn't accept a king over all England. She couldn't give up being called Your Highness. Arthur told me that Father died nobly."

Gaheris hesitated, then added gently, "You may not have heard this before, but Arthur says your father died well, too. He told me that when the battle was over and they saw King Lot and Duke Idres lying together, knights from both sides wept."

Lynet looked down. "I hadn't heard. Thank you,"

she said huskily. Gaheris reached over and touched her hand, gently, and Lynet felt stronger. "Go on," she said.

Gaheris leaned back in his chair. "Mother completely forgot us after Father died. She shut herself up in her rooms, casting spells and plotting vengeance. Finally, she left the castle entirely. I was relieved, but Agrivaine and Gareth still mourn her."

Suddenly Lynet remembered something. "Oh! Back at Sir Persant's camp, when Gareth was wounded and began to call for his mother, you told him — you said she was gone, and he'd better get used to it. I thought that was cruel at the time, but now I understand."

"Ay. Not that it did any good. He'll never see her for what she was."

"And tonight, when you were taunting him —"

"I knew I stood no chance with him in a fair fight, so I tried to make him angry. It almost worked."

Lynet pursed her lips and looked at the grave face before her. She was amazed at Gaheris's strength of mind, the courage to shrug off the knowledge that his own mother had not loved him. It was a sort of courage, she realized, that Gareth would never have. "What happened to your mother?" she asked.

Gaheris frowned. "Gawain says she's dead. He says she tried to kill Arthur but was stopped by a knight from the Other World. I hope he's right."

"What did you do after your mother left?"

"Well, Gawain went to Arthur's court, and a year or two later Agrivaine and I joined him there." Gaheris grinned ruefully. "It was awful."

"Awful? Why?"

"You see, by the time we got there, Gawain was recognized as Arthur's greatest knight. And there I was, his brother, and a clodpole with weapons. Horrible to have to live up to an older brother."

"Or older sister," Lynet pointed out. "I've suffered, too."

"I suppose so. Well, I was young, so I tried to bluff it out."

"Bluff it out?" Lynet repeated.

Gaheris grinned. "Ay. You never heard a knight brag more loudly about what he was going to do but hadn't done yet. I put on the shiniest armor and practiced talking the way I thought knights were supposed to talk —"

"Like Beaumains — I mean Gareth?"

"Well, yes. Like that. But it didn't work for me. After I'd been bashed off my horse in every tournament, by every knight — well, you see my problem. I imagine I looked a priceless ass."

Gaheris shook his head briskly, as if to shake off a bad memory. "Anyway, that's how things were when Gareth arrived at court, the last of the brothers. He was the only one of us who had any of Gawain's skill, but from his first day, Gareth had eyes only for Sir Lancelot."

"I think I know the next part of the story," Lynet said. "Sir Lancelot was defeated in some tournament by an unknown knight with an odd name."

"Sir Wozzell," Gaheris supplied.

"Right. Sir Wozzell. Then Sir Lancelot went away, and your brother followed."

"Something like that. Gareth swore that his name would never be heard again in Camelot until he had restored the honor of Sir Lancelot, and he galloped away in a blaze of glory."

"How was he going to restore Sir Lancelot's honor?"

"Kill Sir Wozzell, maybe. I don't know. Gareth doesn't really think in that much detail. Well, I followed him."

"Because you knew he'd be lost in ten minutes."

"Right. And as I traveled, I met a beautiful woman—an enchantress, you know—riding a white horse. She told me she was lost and fluttered her eyelashes at me and asked if I couldn't guide her to Winchester. I told her I was busy, but I'd be happy to give her directions."

"Oh dear," Lynet said, her eyes twinkling in the candlelight. "I don't suppose she liked that, did she?"

"I suppose not. She said she could never remember

all those nasty directions and fluttered her eyelashes at me again. So I asked if there was something wrong with her eye and told her that I'd once had a horse with a diseased eye like hers."

"You didn't," Lynet moaned, but her eyes lit with laughter.

Gaheris grinned. "I did. That may have been a bit over the top, because that was when she got miffed and cast the spell on me. Hey, presto, I was a dwarf."

"She turned you into a dwarf for that? For laughing at her?"

"Ay. No sense of humor. She said a knight should always treat fair womanhood with respect, and I would remain a dwarf until I'd learned to honor a woman truly. You know the rest. I was only to have my true shape for two hours, every night of the half moon. I don't know why—"

"It's a night for good magic," Lynet explained. "Was it awful, finding yourself a dwarf?"

Gaheris thought for a moment, and said, "A bit of a shock at first, but not all that unpleasant, really. You see"—he licked his lips and frowned—"you see, I'd never been worth much as a knight. But as a dwarf, nobody expected me to be knightly or cared that I was clumsy with a sword. I make a better dwarf than a knight, you know."

Again, Lynet gazed at Gaheris, amazed at his strength of will. Who else would have faced such a fate so coolly? Finally, she said quietly, "Go on."

Gaheris smiled. "I still had a job to do. I was looking for my addlepated brother. It took over a month, but I finally found him. He'd gotten lost in the woods, of course. Even misplaced his own camp, so he'd lost his horse and armor, too. He was half starved and almost out of his wits. Never saw a more pathetic case. Well, the long and short of it was that I took him back to Camelot and left him there, never dreaming that he'd be so daftheaded as to hide himself in the kitchens under another name."

"And you?"

"I rode away. Camelot held nothing for me. I simply set off into the darkest woods, just to see what I'd find."

"And what did you find?"

"A Savage Damsel," Gaheris said, smiling again. "You know the rest."

"Not by half," Lynet said firmly. "How come you wouldn't ride along with that witch, but when you met me, you volunteered to take me to Camelot at once?"

Gaheris rubbed his chin thoughtfully. "I suppose it's because you didn't flop your eyes at me and expect me to roll over. Any other questions?"

"Here's one I've been wanting to ask for weeks," Lynet said. "When you finally got me to Camelot, why did you leave me?"

Gaheris hesitated, then said, "Riding with you was too painful."

"Painful?" Lynet repeated. Her throat was tight.

Gaheris swallowed. "You see, the curse had finally found its mark. I'd found something that I wanted more than anything, but it was something a dwarf could never hope for."

"What?"

Gaheris looked into Lynet's eyes, the lamplight reflecting in twin flames beneath his brows. "You," he said.

"Oh!" Lynet gasped. The night air was suddenly fresh and delicious to breathe.

"Don't say anything, lass," Gaheris said hastily. "I know how things are. I've known ever since Gareth killed the Black Knight. You love him, not me." Lynet started to speak, but Gaheris stilled her with a gesture. "No, you don't have to explain. It was always hopeless for me, and I knew it, even if it tore me apart to think so." Gaheris took a deep breath. "The worst time was the night of the half moon, a month ago. Then I was myself again, and I could do nothing to show you how much I loved you. I slipped out of my blankets and hid in the forest until I'd returned to being just Roger. Those two hours lasted a hundred years.

"Then, the next day, I saw you falling in love with Gareth. I thought I'd go mad."

"Gaheris, I—"

"Ssh! Please! It wasn't that I was jealous—I had no chance with you anyway—but, you see, I knew Gareth. He's never been smart enough or strong enough to love just one woman. I thought maybe he'd changed, when you took care of his wounds at Sir Persant's camp, but then I found him in his tent, dallying with that brainless daughter of Persant's." Gaheris grimaced, with anger and disgust. "In fact, if I hadn't sent you off to check your horse's leg, you'd have walked in on them, too."

"Oh, so that's what—"

"I couldn't take it anymore, watching you in love with him while he was such a—It was more than flesh could bear. So I rode off to take your message to your sister. Just then I didn't much care if I lived or died anyway.

"What else is there to tell? Gareth killed the Red Lands Knight and fell in love with your sister's pretty face, forgetting all you had done for him, forgetting you entirely. Good Gog, I hated him! While he was recovering from his wounds, not a day passed when I didn't think about leaving him to die."

"Why didn't you?" Lynet asked.

Gaheris's mouth was tight. "He's a swine," he said simply. "But he's my brother. You know the rest, up through dinner last night, when he treated you so shamefully. I was so angry that when I took my own form, I thought only of teaching him a lesson."

Gaheris's face was tight and his eyes searched Lynet's. "Don't be too angry with me," he said. "I know you love him, but he's not for you. He's as simple-minded and as selfish and as weak as...as your sister."

"You're right," Lynet said. "They deserve each other."

"They do indeed," Gaheris said soberly. "But you, Lynet, you deserve something better."

Lynet leaned forward, looking into Gaheris's eyes. "I've *found* something better," she murmured, and then she kissed him.

XII

THE HONOR OF
SIR LANCELOT

When she had kissed Gaheris, Lynet straightened up and looked fondly at him while he gaped at her. "Stupid," she said. "It's been days and days since I was in love with your dimwitted brother. His revolting behavior at dinner didn't bother me at all."

"It didn't?" Gaheris whispered.

"Except that when he called Lyonesse his rare golden buttercup it nearly put me off my food."

Gaheris did not move. "You don't love Gareth?"

"No, you idiot. I love you. Shall I kiss you again to prove it?"

Gaheris nodded, and for the next few minutes there was no more talking. When at last their lips were free, they tried putting their love into words. They told each other about the moments when they had first realized they were in love, about the mannerisms and quirks that they found most endearing in each other, and all the usual things that lovers talk about. Lynet reflected privately that if she had overheard the same conversation between two other people she would have considered it appallingly mushy, but it was different when it was just she and her Gaheris.

Eventually, though, Lynet realized that it must be nearing dawn, and they still had a problem to solve. "Gary?" she said. Gaheris had told her to call him by his familiar name. "What are we going to do with you now? If you're found here in the morning, even our witless brother and sister might suspect that you were the midnight attacker."

"Awkward," Gaheris said, nodding. "Shall I hide under your bed?"

"And I could feed you with the leftovers from my meals? What a clever plan!" Lynet retorted.

"Leftovers from *your* meals? Huh! I'd starve," Gaheris muttered. "I suppose I'd better leave. But not far. I won't lose you again."

"You won't," Lynet said firmly. "Can you go back to that cabin where you stayed with Gareth? You could hide for a day or two, then ride up pretending to be searching for Gareth. We could meet for the first time."

"It's too far, and besides, there's no more food there. Don't you have any neighbors I could stay with?"

Lynet pondered this. "They're all tenants on our

land. They'd be sure to tell Uncle Gringamore." Suddenly she smiled. "Except for one. Come on. You can stay with Jean le Forestier."

A few minutes later, they strolled unobserved out the main gate. As soon as they were out of the castle and could talk freely, Gaheris asked, "Who is this Jean?"

"He's a woodcutter. You've met him already once."

"The man who rescued me from Red Lands's guards?"

"That's the one. He saved my life, too."

"Useful chap," Gaheris commented. "Is he really close enough to walk to? Do you know the way?"

Lynet nodded. "I think so."

"You think so," Gaheris said with a sigh. "I have this recurring nightmare where I'm lost in a strange forest, and my only hope is your sense of direction. Enough to give a fellow the sweats, it is."

"Oh, shut up."

"At least I dream about you, lass. Are you sure this is the same woodcutter who saved me? Hairy fellow?"

"That's the one. With dreamy blue eyes."

Gaheris grunted. "I didn't notice his pretty eyes. What were you doing gazing into his eyes, anyway?"

"A lady never tells," Lynet said primly.

Gaheris snorted expressively. After a moment he asked, "How long do I have to stay with this dreamy hairball?"

"Only a day or two, until things settle down a bit."

Lynet hesitated, then added, "No longer than that, please. It will seem long enough as it is."

"Ay, lass. That it will."

To Lynet's relief, her sense of direction did not lead them astray. Just as the sun showed over the dark eastern horizon, they heard the rhymthic sound of an axe on wood. They stepped out of the forest into the small clearing, where Jean le Forestier was splitting logs into kindling. The woodcutter looked up from his work and watched them approach. Behind his bushy beard, his face seemed to clear as he recognized Lynet, but then it clouded again as he looked at Gaheris.

"Good morning, Jean," Lynet said. She plunged immediately into her request. "You'll think me very demanding, I'm afraid, but I'm in trouble, and I've come to ask your help once again."

"I am yours, my lady, to command," Jean said, his face turned to one side. At Jean's voice, Gaheris jumped as if pricked with a needle. "What is your desire?"

"This is a knight of King Arthur's Round Table. He has just been rescued from an enchantment and for his sake — and for mine — he must remain hidden for a day or two. May he stay with you?"

"I am sorry, my lady," Jean said gruffly. "It is impossible."

Lynet blinked with surprise, but pressed on. "He won't take up much space —"

"Quiet, lass," Gaheris broke in, his voice gentle but firm. "Our friend surely has his reasons. Forgive us, sir."

Jean le Forestier reddened behind his whiskers and muttered, "I ask your pardon, but it is not possible that I should have a guest."

"Especially one from Arthur's court?" Gaheris asked, a smile growing on his face. Jean looked sharply at Gaheris. Gaheris smiled more broadly and added, "Whether I stay with you or not, you should know that I will tell no one where you are."

"What are you talking about?" demanded Lynet.

"Then you know me?" the woodcutter whispered.

Gaheris nodded, and Lynet said, "For heaven's sake, Gary, what's going on?"

Gaheris was silent, looking at Jean le Forestier. At last, Jean nodded and said, "You may tell her."

"Lady Lynet, I am honored to present to you Sir Lancelot du Lac."

"I've never really understood why you left the court, Sir Lancelot. Would you explain it?" Lynet asked. They were sitting together on the stoop of the wood-cutter's cottage, watching the woods grow light in the morning sun.

Sir Lancelot shook his head slowly. "I thought — Bah! I was so foolish! — I thought my honor demanded it."

"Because you lost one joust?" Gaheris asked, grinning. "Where would I be if I ran off every time I was unhorsed?"

"Africa at least, *mon ami*," Sir Lancelot said, his eyes brightening. "But it was different for me. I was the one all the young knights admired. I was the one that minstrels sang about."

"I thought you never paid any attention to the minstrels," Gaheris said.

"But of course I listened to them! It was how I knew what to do! They sang that knights wore bright clothing, and I wore bright clothing! They sang that knights were devout, and I took my own priest! Whatever they sang, I attempted. It was the minstrels who created me!"

"I see," Lynet said. "And when they sang that you were the greatest knight in England, you tried to be the greatest knight in England."

Sir Lancelot nodded. "Yes, that's it. And when I was defeated . . . I was no one anymore."

They sat in thoughtful silence for several minutes. Then Lynet asked, "And how did you end up here?"

"It was an accident," Sir Lancelot said. "After I left Camelot, I wandered for many weeks, eating but little, speaking to few, fighting no one."

"Yes, we met one of the knights you didn't fight, a fellow in pink armor."

Sir Lancelot nodded. "Sir Perimones. I liked him."

"So did I," Gaheris said.

Sir Lancelot continued. "At last I came upon a holy man deep in a forest. I stayed with him in his — what do you call it? — *ermitage?*"

"That's it," Gaheris said. "Hermitage."

"Yes. The *ermite* asked if I were a knight, and I told him I was nothing. He said, 'Then you must become something. Learn some work. For in an empty world, you can only find joy in labor.'

"Three days later, weary of traveling, I came upon this cottage, half-built and abandoned. In the meadow I found a rusted axe and an old oxcart. I decided to stay. With the axe, I cut wood and finished the house. Every week I fill the oxcart with wood and pull it to the village to trade for food."

Lynet's eyes widened as she imagined one man pulling an oxcart full of wood all the way to the nearest village, at least two miles away. But, glancing at Sir Lancelot's huge arms and shoulders, she believed it. "And have you found joy in your labor?" Lynet asked.

Sir Lancelot nodded, and for the first time he smiled. "Look at that woodpile," he said. "Every log is chosen well, cut well, of an equal size." He spoke with simple pride. "And at the end of the day, when my arms and shoulders ache and I eat the food of my own earning, I am content."

"More than when you were the greatest knight in England?" Gaheris asked.

"Bah!" Sir Lancelot said, waving his hand in a gesture of dismissal. "To be a knight, it was easy for me. It was as natural as breathing. It is much greater to be the best woodcutter in the forest."

"Do you think you will ever be a knight again?" Lynet asked.

"Why should I?"

"Or I, for that matter," Gaheris said suddenly, a huge smile on his lips. "By Gog, why should I?"

"What do you mean?" Lynet asked.

"I'm no knight. You know that, Lancelot knows that, everyone knows that. I never wanted to be a knight, and I find no...no joy in it. Listen, lass, would you mind moving to the north?"

"What? Why?"

"What I've always wanted to do was manage my family lands — see to the crops, take care of my tenants, put the estates back in good repair, as they haven't been since my grandfather's day. I want to be a farmer."

"But your family lands," Sir Lancelot said, "do they not belong to your older brother?"

"Then I'll get Gawain to send me as his steward. He'll be happy to. He's as unfit to be a landlord as I am to be a knight. How does that sound, lass?"

"Are you asking me to come with you?" Lynet asked.

"But of course I am!"

"Gary, you idiot, you've never even asked me to marry you!"

Sir Lancelot nodded seriously. "You should ask her first, you know. It would be *convenable*—how do you say?—proper."

Gaheris grinned, his cheeks red. "Well, you will, won't you?"

It was not the proposal that Lynet had dreamed of someday receiving, but some dreams are not as important as others. "Yes," she said.

Gaheris smiled warmly, then put one hand on Sir Lancelot's shoulder. "Thank you, Lancelot. You have shown me my honor."

It was evening before Lynet left Gaheris at Lancelot's cabin and walked back to the castle. As she had expected, Lyonesse was waiting for her. Lynet carefully gave Lyonesse the tale that she and Gaheris had concocted for her: how the wounded knight had died and immediately disappeared in a cloud of smoke. Lyonesse looked skeptical. "But knights don't disappear—"

"Oh, he was no ordinary knight," Lynet hastened to explain. "He was a wizard, from another world. Before he died, he told me that he had come to test Sir Gareth. Only the greatest knight in the world could ever withstand him. But Sir Gareth won!" Lyonesse's lips parted and formed an *O*. Her eyes gleamed with pleasure. Lynet quickly followed up her advantage. "That makes Sir Gareth the greatest knight in the world!" she explained, in case Lyonesse hadn't made the connection herself.

Lynet could see that her sister wanted to believe her story, and she sighed with relief. Lyonesse always believed what she wanted to believe. But Lyonesse still had one more question. "But why were you outside the gates?"

"I fell into a trance when the wizard-knight disappeared, and when I awoke I was in the meadow."

Lyonesse's eyes gleamed with credulous awe. "The knight must have put you under a spell!"

Lynet smiled softly. "He surely did," she murmured.

Lyonesse nodded. "Well, you seem all right now. I was afraid you had gone away after that dwarf."

"Dwarf?"

"The one you saved from the dungeon; he ran away during the night." Lyonesse snorted. "That's how he thanks you for your pains. I hope now you've learned what comes of that sort of friendship."

"Yes, I have," Lynet said meekly.

At dinner that night, Lynet was relieved to see that Gareth was none the worse for his night's adventures. He didn't even limp. Before the first course could be served, Lyonesse had launched into a much embroidered version of Lynet's story about the magician.

When she got to the part where the fictional magician proclaimed Gareth the greatest knight in the world, her voice quavered with triumph. But she met with unexpected opposition. Gareth exclaimed, "It is not so! There is but one knight who can ever bear that title — Sir Lancelot!"

Lyonesse was too surprised at being contradicted to answer at first, and Sir Gringamore stepped into the awkward silence. "Well, well, that may have been true a year ago, but Sir Lancelot's gone now. Perhaps he's dead."

"It is not so!" Gareth repeated, even more hotly. "There is no knight who could defeat him!"

"What about your brother, Sir Gawain?" asked Sir Gringamore. "I remember when he was the one called Arthur's greatest knight, and there are some who say that he was always better than Lancelot."

Gareth stood abruptly, knocking his chair down behind him. "They who say so lie! I shall restore Sir Lancelot's honor! You'll see!" In high dudgeon, Gareth stalked out of the hall. Watching him, Lynet could only shake her head. For Gareth, she realized, honor was tournament victories and shiny armor; he would never understand that his hero had discovered honor in sore muscles at the end of a long day of labor done well.

CRUMO

The next day, Lynet rose at dawn, saddled two horses, and rode to Lancelot's cabin. Gaheris was waiting, and after he had embraced her, he muttered, "I thought you'd never get here, love. Did you have to laze about in your bed so long?"

"I'm a lady of leisure, I am," Lynet said, snuggling her head against Gaheris's chest. "Would you like to go for a ride with me?"

Gaheris grinned at the second horse. "You seem sure that I'll say yes. What if I don't feel like riding?"

"Then I'll make you. Remember, I'm better with a sword than you are."

Gaheris mounted with a sigh. "It's a terrible shrew I've chosen for myself."

Lynet smiled, but with a touch of seriousness. "Indeed, Gary, I think you have."

Gaheris reached across and took her hand. "Do you see me trying to back out? You're the woman I thought I'd never find."

Lynet blushed with pleasure, but her face remained serious. "There's more, though. You should know that since you met me I've become a —" The word would not come.

"An enchantress?" Gaheris said gently.

Lynet nodded. "Your Aunt Morgan taught me. I'm a sorceress, like your mother."

"No!" Gaheris said vehemently. "Not like her at

all! If anyone's like Mother, it's your selfish witch of a sister."

Lynet said faintly, "Then you don't mind that I'm an enchantress?"

"My love, I wouldn't mind if you were a kitchen maid. In fact," Gaheris added thoughtfully, "once we're married, you will be. If I have you working in the kitchens, I can get rid of one maid and save money on wages."

Lynet's eyes gleamed. "You do that, but mind what you eat. I know a wonderful recipe for turning people into spiders."

"Huh! Morgan *would* teach you that," Gaheris grumbled. He had not let go of her hand, and it felt comfortable that way, so for the next two hours they rode hand in hand through the welcoming forest. They talked often, and just as often were silent, but their hands were seldom apart.

At last they turned back toward Sir Lancelot's cabin. Taking a short way through the forest, they came upon a meadow, and in the meadow was a knight on a huge black horse. The knight was fully armored, and his visor hid his face, but as soon as Gaheris saw him, he chuckled and said, "Well, of all people!"

Lynet had drawn into the shadows to let the stranger pass by, but at Gaheris's words she said, "Do you know this knight?"

"I'd know that devil horse anywhere," Gaheris said

lightly. He urged his horse forward, out of the trees, and called out, "Hallo, Gawain! You lost?"

The knight turned and removed his helm, revealing an open, friendly face that was at the same time somehow wild and untamed. "Gary?" he said. "Good Gog, Gary, I'm glad to see you!"

While the two brothers embraced with obvious affection, Lynet stared with awe at Gawain, the great knight whose exploits had been told in banquet halls almost as long as she could remember. He was a mountain of a man, but his eyes were kind and reassuring. "Gawain, this is Lady Lynet of Perle. I'm going to marry her."

Lynet rode forward, a bit shyly. Gawain greeted her warmly, and with great grace and even greater sincerity kissed her hand and declared himself her servant. It was quite the most courtly and gracious greeting that Lynet had ever received. Gaheris cuffed his brother on the shoulder and said, "Enough of that, now. What are you doing in these parts?"

"Well you should ask, you bothersome puppy," said Gawain with a snort. "I'm looking for you and your witless brother."

"He's your brother, too, I believe," Gaheris pointed out.

"Not when he acts like a ninny. Well? Is Gareth here?"

"Ay," Gaheris said. "He's up at the local manor, a place called the Castle Perle."

"No, he's not," Lynet said suddenly. A movement at the far end of the meadow had just caught her eye. A knight in familiar black armor sat on a horse at the edge of the clearing. "He must have decided to take the air, because he's right over there."

Gawain and Gaheris followed her eyes. Gawain called out, "Gareth?"

Gareth rode forward, his hand on his sword hilt. "Is it indeed you, Sir Gawain?"

"A bit formal, aren't you, brother? Yes, it is indeed I. And I'm glad to see you looking so—"

"Silence!" Gareth snapped suddenly. His visor was raised, and his face was taut and unsmiling. "I have heard that you have been declaring yourself a greater knight than Sir Lancelot!" Gareth said belligerently.

"Eh?" Gawain replied.

"That's not what Uncle Gringamore said," Lynet interjected. "He only said that some people had said—"

"It is a lie!" Gareth declared.

"Very well," Gawain said agreeably. "Where have you been keeping yourself, boy?"

"Did you not hear me, Sir Gawain?" Gareth snapped. "I called you a liar. Neither you nor anyone else shall declare you to be greater than Sir Lancelot! I have sworn to defend Sir Lancelot's honor at all costs! Draw your sword, Sir Gawain!"

"No," said Gawain.

"Don't be an ass, Gareth," said Gaheris.

Gareth drew his sword and spurred his horse forward, shouting, "For the honor of Sir Lancelot! I shall prove thee no match for him!"

Lynet did not see the beginning of the fight. Gaheris grabbed her horse's bridle and turned it sharply away, leading her out of the way of Gareth's headlong attack. When she was finally able to turn around and watch, both Gawain and Gareth had dismounted, and for the third time Lynet watched Gareth attack an opponent who refused to fight back. Gawain parried every attack — although much more easily than either Sir Perimones or Gaheris had — but refused to attack in turn.

"Look here, lad," Gawain was saying. "You don't really think that it will do anything for Lancelot's honor if you kill me, do you?"

"I've sworn an oath!" Gareth said, panting. He redoubled his efforts, but Gawain fended off every blow, seemingly without effort.

"What can we do?" Lynet asked Gaheris.

"What we need is a fish," Gaheris commented lightly. "You don't happen to —"

"How can you be so calm?" Lynet asked. "Those are your brothers."

"Oh, he won't hurt Gawain," Gaheris said calmly. "People like Gawain and Lancelot are naturals, far beyond the reach of the rest of us."

"And what if Gawain hurts Gareth?"

"I've got no problem with that. I tried to hurt him myself just a couple of nights ago."

"But that was because you were jealous," Lynet said. "Now you aren't. Please try to stop him."

Gaheris shrugged in careless acquiescence and rode a few steps forward. "Gareth, listen. What if Gawain were to write a note saying that he believed Lancelot was the world's greatest knight? You'd do that, wouldn't you, Gawain?"

"Sure. No skin off my nose," Gawain said.

"It is not enough!" gasped Gareth. "I must restore Sir Lancelot's honor!"

Gaheris threw up his arms in disbelief. "And how do you think you're going to do that, you crack-brained block? Kill your brother? Listen, you bed-wetting sapskull—"

"Does he really wet the bed?" interrupted Gawain. "I never knew that."

"You never had to share with him. Don't interrupt, now—"

Gareth swung a mighty blow at Gawain, his breath coming in great ragged gasps. Lynet felt her heart go out to him. His odd notions of honor had trapped him. First, they had led him to make a silly vow; now they wouldn't let him forget it. He'd never rest until he convinced himself that he'd fulfilled his oath.

"Look here, Gareth," Gaheris was saying. "Lancelot

doesn't need you to save his honor. Just because one knight unhorsed him doesn't mean—"

"And it wasn't even me," Gawain pointed out, dodging a ponderous chop. "It was that chap Sir Wozzell."

The answer came to Lynet in a flash. "What did you say, Sir Gawain?" she called out. "Sir Wozzell? How do you know about Sir Wozzell?"

"Sir Wozzell was the, ah, the foreign knight who defeated Sir Lancelot," Gawain said.

Lynet gasped, as if utterly astonished. She could feel Gaheris's eyes on her, but she did not look at him. "But . . . Sir Wozzell . . . that was the name of the knight you defeated the other night, Sir Gareth!" Lynet declared.

There was a sudden silence. Gareth stopped, almost in midswing, and stared at Lynet. A slow grin spread across Gaheris's face, and he lifted his voice proudly. "Don't you see what this means, lad? It means that you have already restored Sir Lancelot's honor! You have fulfilled your vow!"

Gareth collapsed on his knees and lifted his face to the sky. "Thanks be to Heaven!" he said reverently.

There was no longer any point in waiting, so Lynet and the three knights rode to the Castle Perle together. When Lyonesse realized that Gareth's brothers, especially the famous Sir Gawain, had come to her castle, she was almost beside herself with delight and ordered a banquet prepared at once.

At the banquet, Gareth provided the entertainment, telling the tale of his adventures. Lynet could follow the basic events — Gareth's battles with Sir Kai, with the band of thieves, with the black and green and pink and blue knights, and of course with the Knight of the Red Lands — but beyond that outline, she recognized little of the story. Gareth's account had little room for anyone except himself. Only by one or two casual references could a careful listener know that Lynet, and an unnamed dwarf, had accompanied the hero. Gaheris, who was supposedly hearing the story for the first time, clearly thought it was great fun, and Lynet had to avoid Gaheris's eyes if she was to keep from giggling.

Only after the banquet had drawn to an overdue conclusion and everyone had purportedly gone to bed could Lynet and Gaheris meet with Gawain and tell him the true story. He enjoyed it immensely. He did not seem at all surprised to hear about the role that his squire Terence had played, and he knew the little elf Robin well. Only one detail did Lynet and Gaheris leave out: the true identity of Jean le Forestier.

It was almost dawn before Gawain and Gaheris went to their beds, but Lynet was filled with that same magical wakefulness that had kept her up on the night of the half moon. Following some undefined impulse, she left her room and walked out into the night, toward Sir Lancelot's cabin. She had not gone twenty yards past the gate before she was aware of a presence beside her. "Robin?" she asked, unperturbed.

"The same, my lady," came the reply. "You've done well. I told you that you had potential."

Another voice, from her other side, chimed in. "He's right," he said. It was Terence. "We at the Seelie Court are proud of you."

Lynet blushed in the dark. "Thank you. Squire Terence — your grace, I mean —"

"Just 'Terence' is fine," the squire said.

"Did you know that Sir Gawain is here?"

"So I hear. Perhaps I'll come join you at the castle when it's light. I've missed him while he's been away."

They walked together in pleasant quiet through the meadow and into the forest. "Do you know where you're going, my lady?" asked Robin.

Lynet nodded. "I want to thank Jean le Forestier — Sir Lancelot — again. Gaheris and I will be going north soon, and I don't know if I'll ever see him again."

"Oh, I wouldn't worry about that, my lady," said Robin with a merry chuckle. "Lancelot's story isn't over yet."

"No one's story is over yet," Terence said quietly, and the first cool rays of sun began to filter through the woods where they walked.

Epilogue: The Savage Damsel and the Dwarf

Thus did Sir Gareth, whom Sir Kai had called Beaumains upon scorn, achieve his mighty quest. For he slew the Knight of the Red Lands, one of the most perilous knights alive, and by dint of a mighty battle with a wizard named Sir Wozzel in the night, did restore honor to Sir Lancelot du Lac.

In the fullness of time, report of these matters came to Camelot. The whole court of King Arthur was sore astonied when they heard that the kitchen knave they had known as Beaumains was none other than Sir Gareth, but the king was wonderly pleased at the report of Sir Gareth's victories. He declared a great tournament in Sir Gareth's honor, and all the knights of the land came to vie with each other for the prize. Only Sir Gaheris, the older brother of Sir Gareth, did not compete. "No thanks," quoth Sir Gaheris. "Tournaments are boring, and I always lose anyway."

Sir Gareth did many great deeds in the tournament, and when the day was done, he was given much worship. The next day, to the joy of all Arthur's court, Sir Gareth was wed to the fair Lady Lyonesse of Cornwall. All who beheld the couple declared that ne'er had so handsome a knight wed so beautiful a maiden. At the same time, Sir Gaheris was wedded to the Lady Lynet, younger sister to Lady Lyonesse. They looked all right, too.

Sir Gareth became renowned among all King Arthur's knights, for not only was he skilled with lance and sword, but he was replete with all the graces and courtesies of chivalry. Lady Lyonesse, too, became well known. Of all the ladies of Camelot, only Queen Guinevere herself was held in greater honor.

As for Sir Gaheris and Lady Lynet, they left the court and moved far away to lands in the north. Lady Lynet was reported by some to be an enchantress, but few believed these tales, for she never was known to have done any great magical deeds, save only healings of the sick. Sir Gaheris became the steward of all his brother Gawain's lands. These estates were known in time to be the best kept lands in the kingdom, but many in the court considered Sir Gaheris mad. It was unseemly, they said, for a knight to concern himself with such matters as farming.

Those who wondered at Sir Gaheris's behavior kept their counsel, however, for cause of Sir Gawain. Though the great Sir Gawain showed little interest in his famed brother Sir Gareth, he loved Sir Gaheris greatly. At least twice a year, Sir Gawain and his squire Terence traveled to the north for a long visit with these two, whom Sir Gawain did mysteriously call "The Savage Damsel and the Dwarf."

Author's Note

When Sir Thomas Malory wrote his great collection of Arthurian tales, *Le Morte D'Arthur,* the world of books was just beginning. It was 1485, the printing press was still a new invention, and readers were neither very sophisticated nor very critical. As a result, Malory could get away with some things that a modern writer would never dream of doing. A modern writer usually makes all the parts of his or her story fit together, but Malory was unconcerned with such bothersome matters. He did whatever he wanted and offered few explanations.

Nowhere is this tendency more apparent than in Malory's story of Sir Beaumains and Dame Lyonesse in Book VII of the *Morte.* In this story, a skilled knight called Beaumains conceals his real name and takes a menial job as a kitchen servant — curious behavior that would normally call for some explanation, but Malory never explains. Then, when Beaumains rides off on his quest, he is sometimes accompanied by an unnamed dwarf who knows his true identity, but Malory never bothers to tell who this dwarf is or how he knows Beaumains or why he cares to ride with him. After Beaumains arrives at Lyonesse's castle, a knight with no name appears from nowhere and fights Beaumains for no apparent reason. The nameless knight is defeated, but luckily for him, Lady Lynet appears on the scene and magically cures him, although Malory had not mentioned until this moment that Lynet was an enchantress. Indeed, a modern reader's response to Malory's tales will often be, "Huh?"

It hardly matters, though. Despite his peculiarities, there is no one like Sir Thomas Malory. To read his book is to enter a splendid, magical, and unfamiliar world. There is some silliness in that world, to be sure, but there is also honor, sacrifice, and love, all presented in Malory's wonderful language. In the *Morte*, people are not "named," they are "y-clept"; a skilled knight is "passing strong"; a villainous or cowardly knight is a "recreant"; and when someone is very grateful he says with simple dignity, "gramercy."

It is a pure pleasure and an honor to retell this story from Malory's world, to fill in some of the gaps, and maybe turn a few things upside down. And if I've meddled with Malory somewhat, it has always been with affection and with gratitude to him for creating that world that inspires my own imaginings. Gramercy, Sir Thomas.

—Gerald Morris